BAKER'S DOZEN

WENDY SMITH

Edited by LAUREN CLARKE
Cover Designer BOOKISH GRAPHICS
Photography by FURIOUSFOTOG
Cover Model WEN ROSS

ISBN 13: 978-1-991303-05-9

❀ Created with Vellum

GLOSSARY

Moko - Short for Mokopuna. Meaning grandchild.
Weta - A sometimes large insect, native to New Zealand
Ute - Utility truck
Nappy - Diaper

If there are any other words in here that you need help with, contact me and I'll translate. ;)

GINNY

"Do you, Drew Jason Campbell, take Hayley Louise McCarthy to be your wife?"

Drew grins. "Oh yes, I do."

I chuckle, along with the rest of the congregation. Even though I've never met them before, I can feel there's so much love in this ceremony. It's probably the biggest wedding Copper Creek's ever seen.

"Do you, Hayley Louise McCarthy, take Drew Jason Campbell to be your husband?"

"I do."

Wiping my eyes, I look around. Max waves from his post on the groom's side. He's standing with his father, and the two of them have the biggest grins on their faces. It's a beautiful ceremony. I give him a small wave in return.

Next to them are the other three Campbell brothers: Owen, Corey, and James. Max has told me all about them at school, and I think I know far more of that family than I should.

I look a little too long, and Owen's eyes meet mine. Blushing, I look away. I can't help it. I've heard all about the reputation of the town baker, and I'm not interested in just a hookup, but he's still heartbreakingly hot.

I've been so pre-occupied looking around, watching the family I know so much about, I miss the rings being exchanged, but I don't miss the celebrant holding out her hands and smiling. "Go on, Drew, kiss the bride. We know you've been waiting."

Drew pulls Hayley into his arms, and my grin grows bigger watching him kiss her. Love is a beautiful thing, and when it radiates from two people like it does from them, it's something special.

When he leads her out and the wedding party follow, it's like Owen Campbell's noticed me for the first time, and maybe he has as he fixes his gaze on me while trailing along behind his brothers.

The bakery isn't a place I visit. Health issues keep me on a gluten free diet. It eases the symptoms. Doesn't mean I can't enjoy the view of the baker. Maybe I could eat a little.

I stand, and follow the rest of the congregation to the massive marquee that's been set up near the trees. The cove is a beautiful place for a wedding, and it's such a lovely sunny day with no wind. The conditions couldn't be better.

There are a lot of out-of-towners at this wedding, and the businesses in town have geared up for a big weekend. From what I've heard, Hayley's dad is some bigshot, and a chunk of Auckland has relocated to Copper Creek for the wedding.

When I find the little card with my name on it, I sit at the table. The bridal party are having photos down near the water, and I can see them posing from a distance. Laughter floats through the air from them, and it makes me smile.

The water glitters in the sunlight, and I take a deep breath. I come from a small town, but there's something special about this place.

I pick a glass of sparkling wine from a tray and take a look around. The table I'm at is all names I don't recognise, but I'm not far from the bridal table which makes me feel incredibly honoured.

Big social situations make me nervous. I might be a teacher and surrounded by kids all day, but they're easy to deal with compared to a lot of adults.

The chatter increases as the bridal party makes it into the marquee, and I smile as I catch sight of Max.

"Ginny, I'm so glad you could make it." Lily greets me as she approaches, the bride beside her. "I'm not sure if you two know each other. Ginny, this is Hayley. Hayley, this is Ginny. She used to be Max's teacher."

Hayley's eyes widen. "The famous Ginny who Max wanted desperately on the guest list?"

I laugh. "I guess so."

"We told him he could invite one person thinking he'd invite a school friend, but you were the only one he wanted. It's great to meet you."

"You too. It's been such a beautiful wedding."

She grins.

"There she is." Drew draws up beside her, wrapping his arm around her waist. He gives Hayley a lingering kiss that makes me blush.

"Babe, this is Ginny. Max's teacher."

He raises his eyebrows. "*The* Ginny?"

Lily laughs. "Stop it you two. You'll give Ginny a complex."

"Oi. You lot. Time to get seated." Owen walks over and ushers Drew, Hayley, and Lily back to the main table. He shoots me a grin over his shoulder, and I swear I melt into a puddle.

"Miss Robinson." Max comes running over, and I can't help but smile at his infectious enthusiasm.

"Hey, Max. You did well today."

"Did you know there's chocolate cake?"

I laugh and shake my head. "I didn't, but I guess I do now."

"Max." Adam beckons his son.

"See ya." Max runs to him, and I watch as he's led to his seat, a huge grin on my face. He waves at me again, and I can't help waving back. Of all the kids I've taught, it's Max who makes me proudest.

Owen Campbell's looking at me again. I blush as I meet his gaze, but then it could be someone behind me he's smiling at. Among the congregation are some pretty gorgeous girls. I don't recognise any of them as being locals, but then again, I do tend to keep to myself.

Today I made an exception for an exceptional boy.

WHEN THE MEAL'S nearly over but the wine's still flowing, Drew taps the side of his glass with a spoon. A hush falls over the tent, and I turn my chair to get a better view of the bridal table.

Drew smiles. "We're going to make this quick as I'm sure everyone wants to get back to the food and drink. I just want to thank my brothers for standing with me today, and Maxxy. You're the bomb."

I grin, and Max cheers.

"A special thanks to Owen for the wedding cake. Hayley knew exactly what she wanted, and you did such an amazing job."

The cake's wheeled in, and it's gorgeous. Intricate patterns in the icing make it way too pretty to eat, but given that it's chocolate, I might break my own rule and have a tiny piece.

"I want to thank Hayley's parents for this amazing day. I'm so proud and happy to be part of your family. And last, but most important of all ..." He pauses, and looks down at his bride. "Meeting you is the best thing that's ever happened to me. My heart wasn't whole until now. I'm the luckiest man on the planet to be married to you, Hayley, and I promise to love you each and every day for the rest of our lives."

I pick up a paper napkin from the table and wipe my eyes.

"Now, get back to eating and drinking, and we'll start the music shortly."

At one end of the marquee is a temporary dance floor, and when the food's been eaten, we all make our way over to see the bride and groom's first dance.

The band plays something sweet and slow as Drew and Hayley lose themselves in each other. I'm a little envious of their locked gaze. Surely nothing and no one can break that, and although I don't really know them, I hope it continues the rest of their lives.

Slowly, the floor fills with other couples, and I find a seat nearby and sip my champagne.

I can't complain about being lonely when it's my choice, but seeing so much love in the room leaves my heart aching a little. Though, that could be the wine.

The music speeds up, and I close my eyes.

"Dance?"

I open them to see Drew standing over me, his hand extended.

"Me?"

He laughs. "Hayley's taking a break, and she spotted you here by yourself. Thought you might fancy a spin around the dance floor."

I grin. "Why not?"

Taking his hand to stand, I follow him to the centre of the dance floor. Adam and Lily are there, along with Drew's oldest brother. He's really tall and a bit scary, but he has a big grin and a gorgeous blonde hanging off his every word.

"Do you know everybody?" Drew asks.

"I know Lily and Adam."

He nods. "This is Corey, and …" Leaning over, he places his hand to cup his mouth. "I have no idea what her name is. I think he just picked her up."

I laugh.

"Having fun?" Lily takes my hand, and I nod.

We dance for a while before I excuse myself to get some more wine. One more is my limit. Any after that I'll be walking home.

Hayley joins her husband again, and leads him to the cake. Another tap on a wine glass quietens everyone down.

"I just wanted to say thank you again to everyone for coming, and to Owen for this magnificent thing that Hayley doesn't want to cut," Drew says.

Laughter fills the large tent.

"Make sure you get some." I look up to see Owen walk past as he shoots me a wink. I nod, and laugh as he takes the knife from Drew's hand. "I'll cut the cake with you if Hayley doesn't want to."

Hayley laughs, slapping him on the arm.

He holds the knife up as if in surrender. "Okay. You do it. But I want a big piece."

After they make their slice and feed each other cake, Owen takes over and slices pieces from it, giving small plates to Max to deliver.

Max heads straight for me. "Owen said this piece is for you."

I nod. "Thank you, Max."

He beams before heading to the next person, and I get a better look at the icing. Tiny swirls form hearts all over it. It's so delicate and light, but exquisitely detailed. It's a work of art.

I take a tiny bite. The chocolate mud cake melts in my mouth, and I can't help but groan at the taste and sensation. This is a cake made with a lot of love and care. I eat it slowly, savouring each bite. I can't remember the last time I ate cake. It's not part of my strict diet, and I rarely break it. This is worth it.

The music starts back up, and I look over toward the cake. Owen's not standing beside it anymore, and all I'm left with is the hope I can tell him what an amazing job he's done.

Then I spot him.

My heart melts at the sight of Max and Owen in the middle of the dance floor. Max is full of life and laughter, and his uncle seems to have just as much energy.

Max's eyes light up when our gazes meet, and he makes a beeline for my table.

"Come and dance with us, Miss Robinson."

I grin. "I don't know, Max. Looks like you two are having a lot of fun already."

Owen comes up behind him. "What are you doing, Max? Abandoning me in the middle of a dance?" He shoots me a smile. "Hi."

"Hi. Max is just trying to convince me to dance with you guys."

"You totally should. Owen Campbell." He holds his hand out for me to shake.

"Ginny Robinson." I take hold of his hand, and he pulls me to my feet.

"Now you're standing, that's halfway to the dance floor."

Max giggles. "Come on."

"Okay." My hand is still in Owen's as he leads me back to the empty spot, and he reaches for Max's with the other.

Max resists taking Owen's hand, twisting and turning. His excitement is contagious, and I find myself sneaking peeks at Owen who's smiling just as much as Max is.

"Are you having fun?" Owen asks.

"It's been a lovely wedding. The cake was wonderful."

"Thank you."

"I invited her." Max pokes his tongue out.

"Did you? Am I holding hands with your date?"

Max laughs and shakes his head. "Miss Robinson was my teacher."

"Ohhh, so this is the *famous* Miss Robinson. Max talks about you all the time." I laugh, as Owen twirls me under his arm, and I swing one way and then back again.

"Max was one of my best students. Weren't you, Max?"

He nods. "Mum says Miss Robinson is the best teacher I've ever had. But she's not my teacher this year."

Max left me at the end of last year to go to high school. When I came to town three years ago, he was struggling, but I don't think anyone had dealt with a child like him before. Max was behind in his learning, and from what I could see of his school records he'd had difficulties all the way through.

From talking to Lily, he'd had a premature and difficult birth which had influenced that. I took Max under my wing, and we made more progress in two years than he had since he started school. I worried he'd slip at high school, but from the sound of it, he's showing everyone what he's made of.

"You two should get married," Max declares.

My mouth drops open, and all Owen does is chuckle.

"Why's that?" he asks.

"Because then Miss Robinson could be my auntie."

Owen's eyes sparkle, and my stomach flips. I didn't come to Copper Creek looking for a hookup. I kept to myself after a bad breakup. But maybe he could be the man to make me change my mind.

"That's not quite how it works, Max. Miss Robinson and I don't really know each other." He ruffles Max's hair. "Thanks for looking out for me though. Maybe when you're older, you can be my wingman."

"What's that?" Max asks.

Owen grins. "Go ask your father."

Max disappears in an instant, and I gape at Owen. "Poor Adam."

He shrugs. "It comes with the territory. He's just lucky I don't explain sex to Max."

I laugh. "I'm pretty sure he's got some ideas about that. He is in high school."

"Sometimes I forget how old he is."

Owen's phone beeps and he pulls it out of his pocket. His eyebrows dip.

"Is everything okay?"

He shakes his head. "There's been an accident just outside of town. Car versus truck. I've got to go."

"Is it someone you know?"

Owen shrugs. "Not sure, but I'm a volunteer for the fire brigade. If they're paging us, it's got to be bad."

I nod. "Go."

"You owe me a dance, Miss Robinson." He takes a step back and turns before I can say anything further.

I'm left standing by myself on the dance floor, with people still dancing beside me.

I look around the room. How many women has Owen been with here? His reputation precedes him, and I'm not sure what to think about that.

If he really meant anything by his words.

2

————

DREW

"Louise? I didn't know your middle name was Louise."

Hayley reaches up and locks her fingers in my hair. "You never asked. And you clearly didn't look at the marriage license application when you signed it."

I grin. "Even after this past year, I still have so much to learn about you."

She shrugs. "You know all the important stuff."

Her grip loosens and her hand drops as we drive past that damn community on the mountain. We're headed to Corey's place for the night. He's staying at Adam's and lending us his house for our wedding night to give us some privacy.

It's not easy when the town is full of family and Hayley's parents' friends.

As it is, her parents are staying with Mum and Dad. God knows what our mothers will get up to, though judging by the way Mum looked by the end of the evening, she'll be home and in bed. We'll go by and visit tomorrow before we head home and then onto our honeymoon.

"They can't hurt you," I say nodding at the huge fence.

"I know I'm safe with you." Her voice is soft. Something bad's going on behind that fence, and she got sucked into it, but no one will ever get the chance to get near her again.

"Always."

She leans over and pecks my cheek.

"Let's go and have our wedding night, Mrs Campbell."

I indicate and pull into Corey's driveway. His house is tucked in off the street, and unless anyone comes looking for us, they'll never know we're here. It's perfect.

When I stop the car, Hayley grabs my hand. "What if I don't want to change my name?"

"You can do whatever you want. I just like the sound of Mrs Campbell."

She leans over, licking her lips. "Just as well I do, too."

I press my lips to hers.

"Come on," I say when we come up for air.

She grins as I open the car door, and she does the same with hers. As she walks up to the front door, I grab our suitcase from the boot of the car. We didn't pack much. Most of our things are still at home waiting for our ten-day trip to Fiji. Just Hayley and me, the sun and sand, and a teeny tiny bikini I managed to convince her to pack. My wife is hot.

My wife.

Locking the car, I follow her, placing the case beside the door as I slide the key Corey gave me into the lock and push open the door.

She shrieks as I scoop her into my arms. Thankfully, she didn't wear a big fussy wedding dress or it'd be a nightmare carrying her through the door. It's fitting and slinky, and I can't wait to peel it off her.

"What are you doing? Aren't you supposed to carry me over the threshold of our house?"

"I'll do that tomorrow. Today, I just want to do everything by the book."

As we step straight into Corey's living room, I pause and close my eyes. It's hard to concentrate when my wife is nuzzling my neck.

I place her on the floor, and she smiles. "So, what's the plan, Doctor Campbell?"

"Why don't we do it in Corey's bed?" The plan was for us to spend the night in his spare room, but a chance to torment my brother is too much to pass up.

Her mouth drops open. "We can't do that."

"Of course we can. It's a bigger bed than that one in the spare room. I bet anything it's more comfortable. Come on."

I fling open the door, and behind me, Hayley gasps.

Corey knew I'd do this.

His room's lit with small LED candles. They're sitting on the furniture, the floor, the window sills. I grin at the sight of a note on the bed.

Knew you'd end up in here. The bed's better. Enjoy, little brother. I put clean sheets on, and they'd better be in the washing machine tomorrow.

I laugh, and hold up the note for Hayley to read. She grasps my arm and leans her head on my shoulder. "This is amazing."

"Even the big, tough loner can be a romantic."

She looks at me with those blue eyes full of love. "I love you."

I drop the note on the floor. "Come on, Mrs Campbell. Let me show you how much I love you."

Her lips are sweet from the wine we've just been drinking. I nursed a glass for most of the afternoon knowing I was driving up here.

I pull back and cast my gaze over my bride.

"You're so fucking gorgeous in that dress."

"Better get me out of it." She's breathless, and I reach for her back zip, slowly sliding it down.

As it drops to the floor, I take a step back.

Underneath the dress, she's wearing a corset with thigh-high stockings. Even in my wildest dreams, I never thought about what I'd find under the white material, and Hayley is perfection.

"Holy shit, princess."

"You like?" She flashes me a shy smile.

"I love. But I'll love it more when you're out of that."

Hayley rolls her eyes. "My husband's only after one thing."

"It's our wedding day. You know that's true."

She laughs as I scoop her up into my arms and deposit her on the bed.

"How the hell do I get you out of this thing?"

Her fingers pinch the ribbon bowed at the top. "Well, you start here ..."

"Do I need scissors?"

"Drew." She laughs.

"Fine, but don't be surprised if I resort to using my teeth."

Hayley screeches with laughter as I bury my face in her cleavage, peppering her breasts with kisses. She reaches for the buttons on my shirt as I tug at the end of the ribbon.

"What do we have here?"

Her lips twitch. "I don't know."

It takes a few moments, but when the bow at the bottom falls apart, I push back the corset, revealing my half-naked wife. She's more beautiful than ever.

"Nearly there," I say.

She smiles, and I pull her to me, claiming her mouth with mine. God, I love this woman. I love her more than I ever thought possible. The best day of my life was the day I met her.

Hayley falls backward on the bed, laughing as she pulls me with her.

I reach for her white lacy panties, pulling them down her legs.

"What about the stockings?"

"They can stay." I grin.

Discarding my pants, I climb onto the bed between my wife's spread legs. The silk of her stockings is soft against my skin as I lie on my stomach and bury my face between her legs. Teasing her clit with my tongue, I stroke her thighs. She bucks under me, moaning and tugging on my hair as she scrapes my scalp with her fingers. I've always loved going down on her, but tonight it's something special. Hayley's no longer just my girlfriend or partner—she's my wife.

I love that.

"Drew," she cries. Every time she calls my name it takes me back to our first time. I longed to hear her cry my name then, and it undoes me even now.

I sit, pulling her into my lap and impaling her on my cock. Hayley gasps, and grips my shoulders. "I love you," I whisper. "So much, princess."

"I love you too." Her eyes fill with emotion, and I don't have to ask to know she's feeling the same way I am. "Husband."

There's nothing that can take the smile off my face in this moment, knowing she's mine and always will be. Hayley came into my life when I needed her, and nothing will ever keep us apart.

Moving slowly, I savour each second. This is the start of our married life, and the continuation of the best relationship I've ever had. Hayley and I are perfect together.

I kiss her, cupping her head in my hands, and giving everything to her. Our kiss continues as I thrust harder, her hips rocking against mine, our tongues duelling.

Hayley's heart was joined with mine a long time ago, but this day is special.

This day we're one.

I drop my head to her neck, nipping at her skin. She gasps, pushing down harder on me until the pressure builds and we're both overcome.

She is me, as I am her.

"Drew," she says softly.

I'm so deep inside her, and I gaze into her eyes as we sit with our legs locked. I don't want to move. I press my forehead to hers. My whole life I've been a romantic, hoping to find the one person I'm meant to live my life with.

Today, I married her.

THESE PAST SIX months we've lived together, but today we can't get enough of each other. I guess it makes sense. Even though we've known for all that time we were it for each other, making the commitment makes things different between us again.

I don't even know what the time is, but it's really late, and we're both in need of sleep.

"Drew." She strokes my face with her palm, and lets go of a contented sigh.

"Princess," I murmur.

"There's something I need to tell you."

I frown at her serious tone. "What is it?"

She licks her lips slowly, and it makes my cock twitch in response. "I screwed up."

Smiling, I kiss her hand. "Whatever it is can't be that bad."

"You know how insane this wedding preparation has been. Mum's been driving me crazy."

I nod. "I noticed her talking about how proud she was of her doctor son-in-law. That's a change of tune since we first met."

Hayley laughs. "I heard that, too."

"So what's wrong?"

"I think I screwed up taking my pill. And, well, you did say you wanted to have babies as soon as possible."

My eyes widen. "You're ..."

"I'm pregnant, Drew. You're going to be a father."

I grin, claiming her mouth with mine and giving her gentle kisses to convey how happy I am.

"Are you sure you're okay with this?"

My grin grows bigger. "Do bears shit in the woods?"

She laughs, slapping my bicep. "I'm happy, too. I had planned to tell you I wanted to go off the pill for a wedding present, but my addled brain had other ideas."

I press a kiss to her temple. "I love your addled brain." Placing one hand on her stomach, I let out a big breath. "You and me. I think we found another puzzle piece."

Tears roll down her cheeks out of nowhere, and I kiss her softly. "I love you, Drew."

"I love you, too. More than anything. I can't wait to tell everyone."

She bites down on her bottom lip. "About that."

"You want to wait?"

"At best, I'm six weeks. I think we should make sure everything's okay first. I know we've both seen things go bad."

She's right, and even though I want to tell the world, I need to keep this to myself for a while.

"Anything you want, princess." I frown. "Hang on. We were drinking champagne at the wedding reception."

Hayley shakes her head. "You were. I had mine swapped out for sparkling grape juice."

My mouth falls open. "You're so sneaky."

"Maybe, but no one worked it out. I just told the caterer wine goes to my head too fast and I wanted a clear mind for my wedding night. She understood."

I grin.

Hayley makes my heart full, but if it were possible, this news makes it swell even further. I've found everything I ever needed in her, and each day gets better and better.

Everything is perfect.

3

OWEN

There's nothing left of the car.

I don't recognise it at first. All I hear is the wailing coming from the back seat. Someone's alive.

Simon Peters pries the back door open, and I peek in to see a young girl in the back seat. It's dark, and I can't see her well, but I manage to get the harness of her car seat open and free her. As we move back into the area illuminated by the rescue vehicles, I hold my breath. She wails in my ear.

I know this child.

She's been in my bakery so many times in the past three years. Her mother came in at least three times a week for bread, and her daughter was always with her. *Cara.*

I look back at the car. The front of it has completely collapsed, and there's no way anyone survived in the front.

"Two bodies."

Instinctively, my hand goes up to shield the child from seeing anything.

"Owen. Take her over there." I have to be guided away, the urge to see Cara overwhelming. Maybe a miracle's happened and she's survived. My stomach churns, knowing that's not the case.

Ava's all tears and snot as she keeps crying, wriggling in my arms. I know she wants down, but I can't let her get back to that car. Not when it's her mother and father still in it.

"Hey, sweet pea. I've got you."

"Mummy." She lets out a heart-breaking wail, and I rock her in my arms. I don't know a lot about kids, but this one needs comforting.

I'm glad I'm holding her and not at the car. Cara and I had a fling nearly five years ago, and she was one of very few women I became attached to. We might have only seen each other in passing since, but the thought that she's gone rips my heart apart.

The town doctor, Joseph Paton, pulls up at the scene.

He comes straight to me.

"Hey, Ava. Let me just have a quick check."

Patting her on the back, he feels up her spine, and I nod. "I think she's okay. Upset, but okay." I nod toward the car. "I think you need to get over there."

He nods. "It might pay to get her out of here. Take her to the fire station and find her something to eat. The last thing she needs to see are her parents being taken out of the car."

"Of course."

It's the last thing I want to see, too.

He heads toward the car, and I give Ava a little smile. "Hey, sweetheart. How about I take you to the fire station and make you a hot chocolate?"

She sniffs. "I want my mummy."

"I know you do, honey, but it's just you and me right now." I wink. "Tell you what, the bakery's between here and the fire station. How about we stop and get a gingerbread man? I'm sure there are some left."

Her eyes widen, and she nods.

"Come on, then."

I don't have a car seat, but there's a picnic blanket in the back, and I fold it so she can sit on it. It's not like I'll be pulled over. The police are distracted.

In the glovebox is a travel pack of tissues, and I pluck one out and hand it to her. "Here you go. Wipe your eyes."

When she's settled, I drive straight to the bakery. There are a few leftover cookies, and I grab the container they're in and offer it to Ava.

She picks out two, and I take her back to the car, driving the short distance to the station. Maybe here we'll find a distraction to keep her busy until someone comes up with what to do with her.

It worries me. She's a little girl who just lost both her parents, and I'm feeding her up on sugar. But what the hell else am I supposed to do?

At least she's not crying right now.

AN HOUR LATER, I sit at the station, the little girl still clinging onto me. Her small arms are around my neck, and I think she's finally fallen asleep.

She's cried twice, called for her mother, and won't let go

of me. I can't blame her. That it's Cara who died makes me want to hold onto her tighter. She's all of her family that's left.

"We managed to get a social worker over from Carlstown. She's here to take the girl."

I look up to see Graham Taylor walking toward me. He's the senior sergeant at the Copper Creek police station, and he's being followed by a tall, blonde woman. She smiles at the sight of the girl in my arms.

"Where's she taking her?"

Graham sits on the bench beside me. "You knew Cara pretty well. Do you know of any family?"

I shake my head. "I know she didn't have any. Her parents both died of cancer. Not sure about Ryan."

"We haven't found anyone yet. No one who will take Ava."

"So what happens to her?"

The blonde woman looks at me. "She'll go to a family for care. Until we can work out a permanent solution."

"What family? Will it be in Copper Creek?"

She shakes her head. "I've got a family lined up in Carlstown. It's the closest we can—"

"The only home this kid has known is Copper Creek. Her parents are gone. You seriously have to take her to another town with no idea what to do with her?"

Graham puts his hand on my shoulder. "Owen, she'll be okay."

"Cara's gone. Everything Ava's known is gone. You want to take even more away from her?"

"What do you suggest we do?"

I shrug. "I don't know. I can call Adam and Lily. They've got kids."

"They do, but they have to be approved carers. Approved by the state."

I roll my eyes. It's so hard thinking of just handing her over. This is the last piece of Cara left in this world, and I'm reluctant to let her go.

The blonde woman reaches for Ava, and despite my feelings, I hand her over. Ava rubs her eyes. "Owen?"

"Hey, little lady." I reach for her hand, and plant a kiss on it. "You gotta go with this lady now, and she's going to take you somewhere you can get some real sleep. And she's gonna take really good care of you, or I'll kick her arse."

Ava smiles, and Graham rolls his eyes. "She'll be fine, Owen."

"She'd better be."

My heart feels empty as they walk away. What that kid will go through is incomprehensible to me. Ava's an only child. Even when my parents pissed me off, I still had my four brothers.

She's alone.

<hr>

It's a little after nine by the time I'm finished, and I head back to the wedding reception just in case there are people around and the alcohol's still flowing.

Part of me wants to drink myself into oblivion after tonight. There'll be somewhere I can crash at the cove, or I could even get Dad back out to get me.

Drew and Hayley are long gone, and I spot Corey in the

corner of the marquee with the blonde still hanging off his every word. Mum and Dad aren't here either, and I assume James is with them.

To my surprise, Adam, Lily, and the kids are still here, but Lily's picking up rubbish and chatting with Ginny while Adam's sitting at a table with Rose and Max.

"I thought you'd be long gone," I say to Lily, smiling at both her and Ginny.

"The caterers left, and the marquee's not being taken down until the morning, so I thought I'd clear some of the paper napkins and cups. They'll end up all over the cove otherwise."

I nod. "Good thinking."

Ginny touches my arm. "The accident. Was it bad?"

I let out a loud breath. "Yeah."

"Who was it?" asks Lily. "Anyone we know?"

I look around. Chances are the news will be around the town by morning. "Cara and Ryan Mitchell."

Lily's mouth falls open. "Both of them?"

I nod. "Their little girl was the only survivor."

The bag in her hand drops to the ground, and she slides her arms around my neck. "Oh, Owen, I'm so sorry," she whispers.

"It's awful. I took care of Ava until a social worker turned up."

Ginny's hand squeezes my arm, and I shoot her a smile to show my appreciation. She doesn't know the history between Cara and me, but she must realise how tough an accident like that is to deal with.

"Is there any booze left?"

Leaning against me, Lily laughs. "There are a couple of cases of champagne in the corner. It's reserved for family."

"I'll grab some to take home, but I'd kill for a drink now."

"Sit down, I'll get you one." Ginny lets go of me, and heads toward the bottles in the corner.

She's wearing a long, deep blue dress that hugs her curves, and I can't help but check out her butt.

Lily drops her arms, following my gaze, and slaps me gently on the bicep. "She's lovely. Not someone I want to see you get your hands on."

I shift my gaze from Ginny to Lily. "That's not very nice."

"Break her heart and I'll break you." She wags her finger at me, and I believe her.

"I've only just met her."

"I know you, Owen Campbell."

"What's that supposed to mean?"

Lily grins. "I can see the look in your eyes. That and your gaze fixed on her arse."

"Nothing wrong with looking."

"No, there's not, but she's a real sweetheart, so none of your love-them-and-leave-them tricks with her."

I sigh. "I promise."

"I'm sorry to hear about Cara. I know how close you were."

Lily knows better than anyone about my past with Cara. Although she didn't approve of our fling, she snorted with laughter when I recounted the story of Ryan catching us. Thankfully, he didn't recognise me, as he only saw me from behind. But that was the first and last time I ever messed with a married woman.

"Thanks. I just can't believe it. We didn't have much to do

with each other afterward, but it's weird to know she won't be around any longer."

"Here you go." Ginny appears with a glass of wine, blushing as she hands it to me. "I guess I should be going."

"Don't. Stay a bit longer." The words are out of my mouth before I think about them. "You owe me a dance, Miss Robinson."

She laughs.

Lily rolls her eyes and pats me on the chest. "We're going to get the kids home. See you tomorrow at our place for a barbecue? Drew and Hayley are heading off first thing in the morning so they can make their flight on time, but we thought we'd get the family together before James goes back to Auckland."

I nod.

She turns to Ginny. "We'd love to see you too. Around midday?"

Ginny nods.

"See you both tomorrow."

Lily waves as she leads Adam and the kids away. Adam carries the cases of wine, leaving the rest of the bottle for me.

And then I'm left alone with Ginny.

I drink the wine in two gulps.

"You really needed that, huh?" she asks.

"Sure did."

"I'll get you another one."

What I want to do is just skull the bottle, but I take the glass she offers. Everything else has been cleared away. The caterers must have missed this, and I'm glad because drinking out of a glass looks so much better than necking the bottle.

I swallow down the second glass. "Let's dance."

"There's no music."

"Sure there is." I pluck my phone from my pocket and load up Spotify. I pick a random radio station, and the marquee fills with soft music.

"What's that?" Ginny asks.

"No idea, but it'll do." I hold open my arms. "Dance?"

She takes a tentative step closer, and I slip one arm around her waist, clasping her hand in mine.

"I didn't think that today I'd end up dancing in a marquee near the beach." Her soft laughter fills the space.

"Neither did I, but today has been full of surprises."

Her smile warms me after one of the toughest nights of my life, and I close my eyes as I pull her close and we dance slowly.

"Thank you," I murmur.

"What for?"

"For being here. For staying. For dancing with me. I needed this."

She sighs. "I'm sorry you had such a rough night. On your brother's wedding day, too."

"Yeah, not ideal. At least I got to see the ceremony. I'm so proud of him."

"It was a gorgeous wedding."

I open my eyes and lean back. "I think this is the best part."

Her cheeks flush with colour. "I'm enjoying it, too."

The song finishes, and a new one starts. "It's probably time to go home. I'll be crawling if I keep going. Wine does that to me."

She laughs. "I'll give you a lift. I didn't have a lot to drink, and I haven't had anything for the last couple of hours."

"I'd really appreciate that. Walking home in the dark isn't really my idea of fun. I'll come back and get my car tomorrow."

She nods. "If you want, I can pick you up before going to Adam and Lily's."

"I'd really like that."

"Me too."

4

OWEN

I don't sleep well.

Ginny dropped me off outside last night, and we arranged for her to pick me up to collect my car around eleven. I thought after a few glasses of wine, sleep would be easy to come by, but the mangled mess of the car I saw will haunt me for a long time to come.

That, and the thought of Ava. All she had were her parents. Thinking of her being alone drives a hole through my heart.

It's not fair. None of it is.

There's a knock on the door a little before eleven, and I pull it open, finding a smiling Ginny on the other side. It's like seeing her all over again for the first time, she looks so good. Her dark hair is in a loose bun, and her face is free of makeup. My morning's lit up by her smile. I feel like a mess when she's clearly so together.

"Hey," she says.

"Morning."

Her brows knit. "Are you okay?"

I nod. "Tired. I didn't get much sleep."

She tilts her head to the side. "I'm sure. Do you want to go to this barbecue?"

"Yeah. Food might make me feel better." I give her a smile, but it's strained. She makes me feel like I should be at my best with her, she seems so perfect.

"Have you had a shower?"

I can't resist. "Why? Are you propositioning me?"

Her cheeks flush scarlet and she laughs. It's so endearing that maybe even my stony heart might have dipped. "I just thought it might make you feel better."

Shaking my head, I laugh. "No. I just got out of bed."

"Go and have a shower. I'll wait."

She's right, and we do have time. "Okay. Come in."

Ginny settles in on the couch as I make my way up the hall.

"I'm still convinced this is your way of getting me naked," I shoot over my shoulder.

Her laughter echoes through my small flat. "Okay. You got me. That's why I'm sitting out here."

As I shut the bathroom door, I grin.

I really like this woman.

GINNY DRIVES me to the cove to get my car, and I spend the whole trip acutely aware of the woman by my side.

I don't know her well, but she doesn't seem like the type I usually end up with. Though, that's my own fault. Not wanting to commit leaves me with women who want the same. The occasional fun night with no strings has always been my thing.

There's no way Ginny's like that.

She's all kind of sweet and caring without obligation, and it messes with my head. I mean, I know women like that exist—after all, Lily and Hayley are in my family—but a woman like that who seems to like me is pretty special.

"That shower was a good idea. Thank you."

Ginny laughs. "You didn't need me to tell you to have one."

"Seriously, sometimes I'm like the biggest man-baby, and I just need someone to take care of me." *Shit. Why did I say that?* Surely the quickest way to put her off is to make myself out to be some kind of emotional cripple. Even if I am.

"Everybody needs help from time to time. There's no shame in that."

Her voice is so soft, and it does it for me big time. There's nothing fake about Ginny Robinson. "So, why haven't I met you before? You must come into the bakery. Everyone does."

She shakes her head. "I could eat fresh bread all day, but I shouldn't eat gluten."

"Really?"

"You don't have any gluten-free bread, do you?"

"Uhh." She's caught me out there. "No. I did have some for a while, but there was no demand for it. Maybe if I was in the city, it'd be a product that would sell."

She shrugs. "I guess in a small town, there are less people who need things like that. Mary at the Four Square orders some in specially for me."

For some reason that angers me. I want to take care of

that for her. "If it's from the supermarket, it can't be that fresh. I'll bake it for you." I grin. "Now I know I'll have one customer for it."

"You think I'm silly, right? That's usually the first reaction," she says.

I swallow. "No. You said you loved bread. I don't think you'd avoid gluten if there wasn't a good reason for it."

"I'm on a special medical diet, and as much as I hate giving up what I enjoy, I think it helps." A smile spreads across her face. "I did eat that cake yesterday."

My heart leaps. "What did you think?"

"It was beautiful. Hayley was right not to want to cut it, but I'm glad she did. It tasted almost as good as it looked." She looks around. "Where's your car?"

I look up. We're at the cove, and there are a few cars scattered around where we all parked last night, including Corey's truck. I smirk at the memory of the blonde hanging off him. It's not often Corey ventures out in public, and it's even rarer for him to get laid. To think I went home alone. It's a weird reversal for the two of us.

"Uhh, just over there."

She pulls up beside my car and smiles. "Here we go."

"Thank you, Ginny. I really appreciate it. Maybe I can make you some gluten-free bread to say thank you?"

Ginny beams. "Sounds good."

"It also gives me an excuse to see you again."

Her eyes widen, and I think she gets my meaning. I do want to spend time with her, and it's not about getting laid. It's just about getting to know her. Maybe it's because I've just had a reminder about how short life can be.

"I hope the cake didn't muck things up."

She shrugs. "I don't think so. Plus, it was so worth it. You're an amazing baker."

"That cake had a lot of time and love poured into it. Drew wanted to give Hayley something special, and she's so good for him, I wanted it to be perfect."

"Well, it was. I loved it."

I grin. "I'm pretty sure I could sort out some gluten-free cake if you're interested."

"Very interested."

Leaning over, I peck her on the cheek. She blushes again, and it leaves my heart in my throat. "I'm hoping you're not just interested in the cake."

I leave her in the car, watching me with her mouth hanging open.

Last night was crazy, but Ginny's presence and the ease between us leaves me a little more optimistic about the future.

Maybe she could be exactly what I need.

GINNY FOLLOWS me in her car to Adam's place, and he's waiting in the backyard as we pull into the driveway. I don't know if she notices, but his eyebrows creep up as he watches me usher her through the gate.

"Lily's inside," he says.

She nods. "I'll go and find her."

I love the way she looks from behind. The view is almost as good as it is from the front. She's wearing jeans today, and they accentuate her shape even more than the dress did yesterday.

This feels so much like a date with us arriving together, but I've never brought a date to a family event before. Her presence stirs up mixed emotions—excitement, anticipation, and more than a healthy dose of nerves.

"What's going on with you two?" Adam asks, nudging my elbow.

"Who?" I grin.

"You and Ginny. Arriving at the same time?"

I smile. "She gave me a lift to the cove to get my car before coming over."

"So, you two …"

I shake my head. "No. Lily warned me away from her."

Adam smirks. "Is that going to stop you?"

"Hell no. But then, I guess Lily is right. If I'm going to hurt Ginny, maybe it would be better if I didn't go there."

Adam's smirk's still there, and I punch his arm. "What?"

He leans over. "Seems to me that if you're already caring about her feelings, maybe there is something there. It's not like you."

"I think that's a little unfair."

"Says the man who's left a trail of broken hearts for years."

"I'm not completely heartless, Adam."

He frowns. "Lily told me about Cara and Ryan. I'm sorry, Owen."

"Don't feel sorry for me. It's their little girl I'm worried about. She's gone to stay with a family she doesn't know."

Adam sighs. "Man, that sucks."

"Yeah. I'm trying not to think about it, but it's hard. She went through so much last night, but she was so brave."

He slaps me on the back. "Come on. Grab a beer, and

we'll get this barbecue fired up. Lily's been up for ages getting food prepared."

We walk around the house to the backyard. Corey's sitting on the deck, dark glasses on, his arms folded.

"He arrived and fell asleep about half an hour ago."

"His ute's still at the cove."

Adam chuckles. "He spent the night in some girl's motel room. Doesn't want to talk about it."

"That could be good or bad."

We laugh, and our older brother stirs. He pulls his sunglasses down, peeking over them. "Could you two keep it down?"

"Are you that hungover? Could you even perform last night?" I call out.

"What does that mean?" Max's voice comes from just inside the house.

Adam nudges me as Max appears on the deck.

"Oh, you know, Max. Corey was dancing with a girl last night. I wondered if he'd managed to sing for her, too." I grin.

Adam shakes his head. "You're going to get me into trouble."

"I've never heard Corey sing." Max bounces toward me.

"Me either, bud. Maybe he can sing for us later."

I chuckle as Corey raises his middle finger to me.

"That's not nice, Corey." Max laughs, and runs back inside the house.

"Did you really have to do that?" Adam rolls his eyes.

"It got a great reaction from Corey."

"I'll grab us a beer. Take a seat."

Lily appears in the doorway with Ginny. "What's this about Corey singing for us?"

Adam glares at me. "That was Owen's way of getting out of the hole he'd dug for himself. He said something inappropriate in front of Max."

Lily laughs. "I didn't think it was true. Corey's no singer."

Corey raises his middle finger to her, and we all laugh.

"Come and take a seat, Ginny," Adam says. "We're about to fire up the barbecue."

"Thanks." She takes a seat opposite Corey who sits up straight.

"Hey, Corey. We're in polite company now, so could you please put your finger away." I nod toward Ginny.

"Corey Campbell." He leans forward, his hand extended. "You were at the wedding yesterday, weren't you?"

Ginny nods. "I used to teach Max. Ginny Robinson." She shakes his hand, and my older brother slips his sunglasses off.

"Max talks about you a lot."

"So I hear." She tucks a lock of her long, brown hair behind her ear, and it irks me. Is that a flirting move? With my brother? Do I say something about her being her with me? Only she's not. She just took me to pick up my car.

"Owen, can you help me in the kitchen please?" Lily grabs my arm and pulls me toward the door.

"What do you need?" I ask as I follow her inside.

She stands in front of me, her hands on her hips. "Are you going to let Corey chat Ginny up?"

I place my beer on the nearby table. "What are you talking about, woman? They've just met. Besides, you told me to steer clear of her."

Lily frowns. "I know, but she looks so good with you."

Raising my hands to my face, I cradle my forehead. "Would you make up your mind?"

She pats me on the chest. "You were with her last night, and you're with her now. That must be some kind of a record for you."

I reach for the tea towel sitting on the bench, and she squeals as I flick it at her arse. Laughing, she holds her hands up in surrender. "I'm sorry. I couldn't help it."

"Yes, I like her. Okay?"

Lily grins. "I knew it." There's a wail from the bedroom, and Lily pats me on the chest. "That's your niece finishing her nap. Want to go and get her?"

Rose is a year old now, and has just started walking. I love that little smiling face of hers, and I nod.

"She might need a change of nappy, too."

I shake my head as I walk away. "Now you tell me."

"Hey, it's good practice for the future."

Chuckling as I enter the room, I'm greeted by my beaming niece whose smile lights up the room. She's not cranky about waking up, but she is annoyed she can't get out of her cot.

"There's my beautiful girl. Have you been asleep?" I scoop her into my arms. I'd never admit it to Lily, but if any kid makes me clucky, it's Rose.

"How about we just take a minute before I take you out? I get you all to myself." I hold her tight and breathe in that baby smell she has. Lily was wary of us in the early days with Max, and it took time to gain her trust. With Rose, we've all been there from the start. I don't know if I'll ever have my own children, and that makes these times with my niece and nephew are so special.

"Do you need a bum change?" I feel her nappy, widening my eyes. "Oh, yes you do."

She giggles as I plant her on the change table and reach for a nappy.

"I'm going to take you out to meet Ginny. She's going to love you to bits. I'm going to tell you a secret." I lean over. "I really like her."

"Mum mum," Rose says.

"You'll see her in a minute too."

I pull the drenched nappy off and use a wipe before wrapping the clean one around her. Placing the dirty one in the nappy bin, I pick Rose up. "Let me wash my hands and we'll go outside."

We head to the bathroom, and I place her on the floor while I wash my hands. Scooping her into my arms, I carry her out to the deck. Lily's standing beside Adam at the barbecue, and Rose squeals in my ear.

"Yeah, there's Mum."

Ginny's still having a conversation with Corey, and jealousy rages through me. It's stupid. She looks like she's being polite, and Corey's still hungover and looking like shit. But something he says makes her laugh, and when she throws her head back, it's the most glorious thing I think I've ever seen. There's nothing fake about her. She's beautiful.

I catch her gaze, and she gives me a shy look before returning her attention to Corey.

"Bro." Corey grins. "And you've got my girl?" He reaches for Rose, and she holds out her arms in response. I hate handing her over, but I do.

"What *did* happen to you last night?"

He shrugs. "Nothing I'm going to tell you about."

"Maybe you *were* too drunk to perform." I laugh as he takes a swipe at me, dodging out of the way.

"Corey was telling me a story about you when you were younger." Ginny grins.

I take a seat beside her. "Is that right?"

Corey chuckles. "Yeah. Remember when we were play-fighting, and we broke the coffee table in the lounge?"

"And we decided to glue it back together and not tell anyone?"

He nods. "That's the one. Worked a treat until Mum decided to eat dinner in front of the television and placed more than a coffee cup on the table."

I laugh, now knowing what Ginny had reacted to. "What a mess. I just remember meatballs rolling under the couch from the spaghetti."

"We were scrubbing the carpet for hours."

Ginny touches my arm. "It sounds like you guys were real terrors." Her eyes shine with happiness, and my heart swells.

"There were five boys in our family. That was a recipe for disaster." I feel more settled now I'm by her side again, and I can't explain it.

It confuses me.

By two, I'm yawning my head off. If I don't go home now, I'll be asleep.

"Are we keeping you up?" Corey asks.

"Something like that. I should get going."

Standing, I walk to Lily's chair. She smiles as I bend to kiss her on the cheek. "Thanks for lunch."

"You're welcome." She beckons me closer. "So, you and Ginny?"

"I repeat. You told me not to go there."

"And I told you that you two look good together. Maybe you should." She frowns. "But I still think you'll hurt her. Maybe not intentionally."

"Maybe I'm better than that."

Her eyes search mine, and she gives me a smile. "I know you are. You're a good man, Owen. You just have to reach a point in your life when you're ready. And maybe you just need to meet the right woman."

"What would any of us do without you, oh wise one?" I grin, straightening up.

She slaps my leg. "Smart arse."

"You know it. Catch you later."

Ginny's talking to Adam, and as I approach he nods and walks toward me. "I'm just going to grab another beer. Want one?"

I shake my head. "No. I'm getting out of here."

"See you." He heads toward the house, leaving me with Ginny.

"Are you leaving?" she asks.

I run my fingers through my hair. "Yeah. I think I need to try and get some sleep. After last night, I'm still tired."

"Oh." She tries to hide her disappointment, but not well enough. It makes me smile.

"Thank you for everything."

Ginny shakes her head. "It's no problem."

I want to ask her out, but Lily's words echo in my head. She's right. There's a chance I'll hurt Ginny if I pursue this, and I don't know if I'm in the headspace after Cara's death to deal with anything heavy.

I'll do the mature thing for once and hope she's available when I'm ready.

"See you around?"

She nods. "Sure thing."

When I get to my car, I turn to look back at her. She gives me a wistful smile and walks toward Lily.

Time to go.

5

OWEN

I have two concurrent thoughts running in my head that stop me from sleeping.

One is about Cara. It's the funeral today, and I think there'll be quite a lot of people there. When it became clear that neither her or Ryan had their shit together, the community raised the money for the funeral in record time. I can only hope that social worker has the decency to bring Ava. That little girl needs to be able to say goodbye to her parents.

For my part, I offered to do the catering for free. What's an extra hour of baking for the day when you have insomnia?

But that's not the only thing on my mind.

Green eyes give me comfort. Maybe even hope. Ginny's gorgeous with a sweet smile, and long auburn hair.

But it's her sweetness that draws me in, the way she blushes when I look at her. I've been with a lot of women in my life, and usually they're as brazen as I am. Ginny's not like that, and it intrigues me.

Although, it could also be that with Adam and Drew settled, I'm a bit restless. If things are working well for them, is it time to find the right person and sort my shit out?

Who knows?

In the meantime, I'll be focusing on the food for the funeral. I'll even make some of my famous gingerbread men just in case Ava's there.

Mel leaves me alone while I'm baking. Usually we're in there together, but she knows how hard today will be on me.

I'd be lost without her. My last apprentice moved away halfway through his training, and Mel showed up, wanting a job and eager to learn. She's also one of the best friends I have. It's like being married but without all the crap that goes with it. Besides, she's married to Trish, and there's no risk of us screwing up our friendship by sleeping with each other.

"It's nearly time," Mel says gently, and I nod. The food's all boxed up, and I just need to transfer it to the car.

We work in silence, and I smile as we load the last box. "Are you sure you don't want to come? We can just close the bakery for a bit. No one will care."

She shakes her head. "It's okay. I'll hold the fort."

"You're amazing."

"You should give me a pay rise then."

"Maybe I'll get off my arse and employ someone to help you instead."

She laughs. "That'll do."

"Thanks for your help, Mel. I really appreciate it."

Mel pats me on the back. "No problem. I know how important this is to you."

"See you later."

I climb into the car and drive the short distance to the funeral parlour. There's a reception room next to the chapel, and I carry the boxes of food in and set it all up on the table. I can hear cars pulling into the car park, and I pause to take a deep breath. This is it. *Goodbye Cara.*

I walk back out and into the gathering crowd.

There's no sign of Ava, and I hunt for Graham Taylor. He's standing by himself, looking up at the sky as if he's wishing he was anywhere but here.

"Graham."

He shifts his focus to me and smiles. "Owen."

"Where's Ava?"

Frowning, he shrugs. "I called Marie and left her several messages. Fucking hopeless, if you ask me. Of all the people who should be here, that little girl should be."

"Agreed."

For a few minutes, I wait and watch the entrance to the car park. More cars arrive, this is going to be a big funeral, but there's still no sign of a small blonde girl who's the most important mourner. *Does Ava even really know what's going on?*

People are already filing into the chapel, and I join them. There are still plenty of seats, and I find a row near the back that's unoccupied. Sitting gives me a minute to try and clear my thoughts, but my heart breaks at the sight of the two coffins, side by side.

This is so unfair.

Neither Cara nor Ryan ever did anything to hurt anyone other than each other. Although he suspected, he never caught us, and our fling didn't last long. She was the only married woman I ever got involved with, and he was being a real dick to her at the time. I saw it myself.

Somehow, they worked things out, and I'd vowed never to be with a married woman again.

For a couple who don't appear to have anyone else, it's a big turn-out. I look across the room toward the door and meet the eyes that have haunted my thoughts.

Ginny scans the crowd, as if she's looking to see if she recognises anyone. She might not shop at my bakery, but chances are she shopped at the butcher. Unless she's a vegetarian, as well as not stomaching gluten.

I raise my hand and wave, and a small smile appears on her face. She seems to take a deep breath, and walks toward me.

"Hey."

"Hi, Owen." She takes a seat by my side.

"How's it going?"

She shrugs. "I didn't know Cara and Ryan well, but I used to see one of them at the butchery every week. They seemed so nice. I'm heartbroken for their little girl."

I nod. "Me too. They were good people, and Ava didn't deserve this."

"Where is she?"

I bristle, and she reaches for my hand before breaking into a blush. "She got taken by a social worker to stay with a family out of town. I thought she would have been here. The cops are trying to get hold of the social worker to make sure she's coming."

Ginny's mouth falls open. "You're kidding. The service is about to start. How awful."

I squeeze her hand. "I'm glad you're here. And that you're holding my hand again."

She laughs, but doesn't let go. "I might need some support. Funerals are bad enough without it being a young couple like this."

"Aren't you supposed to be in school?"

"A lot of the staff wanted to come. So the deputy principal has the students in the hall for a movie until hometime. I guess that's what happens in a tight community like this."

She moves even closer when she spots Nathan Webster in the doorway. He's the principal of the local primary school, and that makes him Ginny's boss. When he sees her, he smiles, and heads straight in our direction, sitting next to us.

Ginny's so close I can smell her scent. It's earthy and faint. She consumes my senses, and just like that, I'm getting hard at a funeral.

"Owen." He nods, and his gaze shifts to Ginny's hand in mine. I tighten my grip and hope it gives her some reassurance. He clearly makes her uncomfortable, given how clammy her palm has become.

"Nathan. I hear you let your staff attend the funeral. That's awesome."

"It's the least I can do. Cara and Ryan were part of so many people's lives." He's still focused on Ginny's hand. We're the only three people sitting in this row, and part of me wants to tell him to fuck off.

"Bro." Adam arrives, breaking the tension.

"Hey, man. Come and sit with us." I move over as far as I can, and pull Ginny with me to leave a gap between her and

Nathan. Thankfully, Adam seems to take the hint and makes his way past Nathan to sit between them.

"Ginny. How's it going?" Adam gives her a warm smile, and as his eyes catch our hands clasped, his brows pop up.

"Good. How's Max doing?"

He grins. "Really well, thanks to you. He's settled in at school, and his teacher is pretty good. But I think you prepared him, and he's benefitting from that."

"That's brilliant."

The remainder of the seats fill, and the doors close. I look around. Still no Ava.

"Are you kidding me?" I mutter.

Ginny turns to me, her eyes full of sadness. She doesn't even need to ask what I'm talking about. She just seems to know. "It's not fair," she says. "Ava should be here."

"This is ridiculous."

The minister steps up to start the service when a door opens. Ava stands in the doorway with big eyes, looking around at the crowd. A tall, dark-haired woman stands beside her, and leads her to a seat at the front.

I let out a breath for the first time in what feels like forever. Now everything is as right as it can be, at a time like this.

The service begins.

IT'S TOUGH.

So many people cry their way through it. Cara and Ryan were a couple in the prime of their lives.

From where I sit, I can see Ava gets upset during the

service, and the woman she's with pulls her into her arms and hugs her.

It leaves me wanting to comfort her, too.

Somehow I get through it. It helps that Ginny still sits beside me, holding my hand. She must feel me shaking at times, struggling to deal with the farewell of a woman I cared for. I'm not as shallow as some people think I am, and I do care about the women I've been involved with. But I'm no good at sticking around.

Lily's warning rings in my ears, but I can't help wanting something with Ginny. I just don't know what yet.

The fresh air outside is a welcome greeting as I step into the sunshine.

"Are you okay?" Ginny asks, her expression full of sympathy.

"Not really." I sigh. "But I'll survive. Thank you for what you did in there."

A smile spreads across her face. "It was nothing. You obviously needed the support."

"I did, and I'm grateful."

Her gaze shifts. "Look. There's Ava."

"Good. I've got something for her."

I jog toward her. She's being led away by the woman who brought her. They're not even staying for something to eat.

Irritation burns in my chest. "Ava."

The woman stops. Ava turns, giving me a timid smile.

"I'm Jackie. Ava's staying with me at the moment." The woman thrusts her hand toward me, and I give it a firm shake.

"Owen." I bend down, taking a small package from my jacket pocket. "Here you go, sweetheart. I brought these just for you." I hand Ava the gingerbread men wrapped in cling-film, and she smiles as she takes them from me.

Jackie reaches down and takes them away. Ava's lower lip wobbles. "Thank you, but we don't eat sugary things in our house."

"She's four, and this is her parents' funeral. Surely she can have a treat?"

"If I let her have this, the other kids will want one."

My anger building, I draw myself up to my full height. "Then I'll give you enough for however many children you need."

She shakes her head and shoves the small package back at me. "No thanks. We don't need it."

Ava looks back over her shoulder as they walk away. Ginny arrives at my side, and nudges my arm. "What was that all about?"

"Ava's not allowed the baking I made her."

"What?"

"The family she's with doesn't eat things like this."

Ginny rolls her eyes. "Leave it to me."

She takes the gingerbread and runs after Ava. "Hey, Ava. Can I please say goodbye? I'm a friend of your mum."

I know my eyebrows are arching more than normal as Ginny squats and hugs Ava tight. Slipping the package between her soft toy and her body, Ginny whispers something in Ava's ear. Ava lights up, and lets Ginny hug her.

Ginny skips back to me. "Sorted."

"What did you say to her?"

"That it was our secret. She has to hide it and not let anyone see it."

I laugh. "You're sneaky, Miss Robinson."

She shrugs. "Ava's been through enough."

If I didn't like her a lot before, I like her a lot now.

Ginny Robinson might just be perfect.

I STAY until I can't stomach any more.

"Want to come back to my place? Given that you don't have to go back to work."

Ginny nods. "Sure. Something tells me you need someone to keep an eye on you. I know today's been tough."

"It really has been."

By the time we reach the bakery, my joy at our little rebellion has dissipated, and the sadness at Cara's passing returns.

"How was the funeral?" Mel asks as I walk in the front door.

"Sad. Big turnout, though. Can you do me a favour?"

"You want me to take care of the shop for the afternoon?"

I press my hands together. "If you could?"

"Knowing what I know, I figured you'd need some time afterward to get yourself together." Ginny walks in the door, and Mel smiles. "Got some company, too?"

"Something like that."

"Good for you. Just don't make too much noise, it's bad for business."

I shake my head at her as I guide Ginny out the back of the shop, through the kitchen and into my flat.

"Your place is so convenient for work."

I nod. "It's handy when you have to go to work at four in the morning."

"Really?" She looks around the living room. It's nothing too flashy, but it's cosy, and I have all the essentials. Comfortable leather lounge suite, big-screen TV. The important things.

I sit on the couch, and pat the seat beside me. "That's the life of a baker."

"I guess I never thought about it." She sits, and smiles at me.

"Truth is that I probably don't quite live the life people think I do. I have to get up way too early to do half the things I'm supposed to have done. This business means everything to me." I nudge her arm. "I'm only sorry you're not one of my customers."

"Well, maybe I can be if you start selling something I eat."

Our gazes are locked, and for the first time she doesn't blush and look away.

"Thank you for coming home with me," I say.

"I wanted to make sure you were okay."

I lean back and close my eyes. "Today was rough. Cara and I, we were together for a while a few years ago."

"Oh, Owen, I'm so sorry." The sympathy's clear in her tone.

"It is what it is. She was happy with Ryan in the end." Tears well, and I can't help it. This whole thing has me rattled. Life's so short as it is, but Cara and Ryan makes me look at my own mortality. What do I have to show for the life I've led other than the bakery?`

"Hey." When Ginny reaches for me, it's tentative at first, but she slowly slides her arms around my neck, and I rest my chin on her shoulder.

"I'm sorry. I think I'm going to be okay, and then it hits me again."

"There's nothing to be sorry about. You're human. It's okay to hurt."

I close my eyes. It pains me to think of what happened to Cara. That her life could end that way hurts more than anything. She and Ryan should have been able to grow old together.

"To be honest, I don't know how to feel. I'm sad she's gone, and I'm devastated for her little girl. What happens to her?" I open my eyes.

Ginny shrugs. "I don't know what the authorities do in these circumstances."

"Neither do I. I do know I'm going to put in a complaint about today. That woman was awful."

She nods.

"Thanks again for your help with Ava. I was so angry."

"I could tell. But you did good. You didn't make things worse for her. I hope she enjoys the cookies you made her."

I smile. "Me too."

Exhaustion hits me. I've been running on adrenalin since the night of the accident. Between not sleeping well and my early-morning starts, I'm more tired than I have been in a long time. I yawn. "Sorry."

Ginny smiles. "It's okay. I should get out of here."

"Stay for a bit longer?" I can't deny I like her company.

"Sure. Maybe you should see if you can sleep." She pats her lap, and I smile, stretching out on the couch and laying my head on her knees. It's intimate, but reassuring. Just what I need. "Tell me about you and Cara."

"Really?"

She runs her fingers across my forehead. "It might help."

It won't win me any brownie points, but for some reason, I feel I can talk to Ginny about this. "She chased me. I gave in eventually even though she was married. We had fun together, although for a while I thought it was a little more than that. Ryan caught us once." I smile. "It was such a cliché. The only way out was the window, and he caught sight of me from behind. I was naked and clutching my clothes, hoping I didn't drop anything identifiable."

Ginny laughs. "Did he ever work it out?"

"Pretty sure he was suspicious. Cara called it off shortly after, said she wanted to work on their marriage. Later on, they had Ava, and they seemed really happy after that."

I close my eyes as Ginny strokes my temple.

"You know, I could get used to this," I say.

"What?"

"You taking care of me."

She lifts her hand. "I just wanted to make sure you were okay."

I open my eyes. "I think I am now, thanks to you. Are you going to let me take you out to dinner to say thanks?"

Ginny shakes her head. "That's not necessary."

I sit, and look into those gorgeous green eyes. "I want to. Not just to say thanks, but because I want to take you out."

"Owen, you don't have—"

"I know I don't have to. The truth is that I have been thinking about you since the day of Drew's wedding."

Her cheeks flush with colour. "I've thought about you, too. I'd heard stories about you, but that whole reception you spent all your time with Max. There were some beautiful women there, but you stayed with your nephew. It was sweet."

"Max is easy to spend time with. That kid is the best."

"He is."

"He led me to you." I swallow hard. Other than with my family, I'm rarely earnest. I joke and I flirt and I tease, but no one gets the sentimental part of me. Ginny's done nothing but show me kindness and give me hope. I'm an open book to her.

"Owen—"

"Just say yes."

"I can't. I told you I heard the stories, and I work with someone you went out with, slept with, and then moved on from. She's still hurt, even though it was a while ago."

"Becky Lake."

Ginny nods. "I work pretty closely with her, and even though she sometimes talks about how being dumped by you led to her finding true love with her husband, Glenn, being with him doesn't stop her from being bitter about the way you treated her."

"You know all that and you still came to keep an eye on me today?"

She licks her lips. "I think you're a nice guy. But I have to be wary. My heart's been battered before, and I don't want to do that on repeat."

I take her hand in mine. "I wouldn't do that to you. Becky isn't the easiest person to be around. She got … clingy."

"Who's to say I wouldn't do that?"

"Would you turn up in my shop and harass an innocent customer because she was dressed for the beach and ask her if she was my latest whore?"

Her eyes widen. "Really?"

"Yes. The poor girl was a tourist, not even a local. She only came in for a croissant. I had to knock that on the head pretty quickly."

Ginny's expression tells me she's torn, and I understand that. She'll have listened to what Becky's had to say, and anything I say to contradict it may not ring true. Finally, she shakes her head. "I won't be another notch on your headboard."

I nod. "I understand. Doesn't mean I'm not going to chase you."

The corners of her mouth turn into a smile.

Game on.

6

OWEN

A SPLASH OF LIQUID HITS ME ON THE CHEEKS.

Waving my hands in front of my face, I try and stop the water being flicked on me. "Cut it out."

Ginny.

The last thing I remember is my head on her lap, her fingernails raking my hair.

Opening my eyes, I expect to see Ginny standing there. Instead, it's Mel, smacking her chewing gum, just like I hate, and standing over me.

"Mel?"

"It's five in the morning. and I've been in that kitchen for an hour by myself."

I sit up. "Shit. I fell asleep."

"Yeah, your girlfriend left like twelve hours ago. Probably just as well, as you were snoring your head off. I think someone had a bit too much to drink."

I bury my head in my hands. That's not a look that's

going to impress Ginny. My head thumps from the half a bottle of whisky I consumed before lying back in her lap.

"It's okay. I think she still likes you. She told me on the way out to keep an eye on you, but when I came in here, you were fast asleep and burbling some crap about how nice she was."

Shit. "I'll just jump in the shower for five and come out."

"Do you know what I think?"

I shake my head and wait for her words of wisdom on my potential relationship.

"You need to get your shit together and get someone in to work afternoons. I'm over this twelve –hour-day bullshit."

I chuckle. Mel's always been upfront with me. I think that's why we get along so well.

"Okay. I'll put a sign up. We'll find someone."

She crosses her arms and nods. "I've already put one in the window."

"See? I knew there was a reason I liked you so much. You complete me."

Leaning over, she cuffs me on the ear. "Stop being a smartarse. You must be losing your mojo. She didn't stay the night." Mel's lips twist. "Mind you, you don't usually bring them home with you."

"I was a bit of a mess after the funeral. Did you know Cara and Ryan's daughter nearly missed the service?"

"Really?"

"You know she's in care? The woman she's staying with ran late, and they arrived just as the service started. I'm not impressed."

Mel takes a seat beside me on the couch. "That's so shit."

"Yeah, but what do you do? It's none of my business, but I'm so angry about it."

She squeezes my shoulder. "Maybe you should talk to Graham Taylor about it. He's got to have contacts that he can pass that onto."

I nod. "You're right. You're always right. If you weren't already married, I'd ask you to marry me."

Laughing, she rolls her eyes. "If only I was into men."

"Well, technically, you don't have a husband, you have a wife, so maybe there's hope for me yet."

She stands, cuffing my ear again.

"Ow."

"Get your arse in the shower and into the bakery."

"Yes, boss."

She laughs as I walk down the hallway, waggling my arse as I go. "Owen Campbell, I don't know how your mother ever put up with you."

"Neither do I," I call over my shoulder as I get to the bathroom.

I've never worked with a hangover, and it shows. I drag my way through the day, and even take a break after the lunchtime rush to have another shower.

I'm dead on my feet by the time we close the door. It doesn't help that a coachload of tourists on a day trip wiped us out. We'll be extra busy in the morning replenishing stock, but that's tomorrow. Today is over and done with.

"Good night," Mel says.

"Did you get any bites for your ad?"

She shakes her head. "Maybe tomorrow."

"We really could use the extra help."

Poking her tongue out at me, she waves as she leaves. It's

something she's been telling me for a while, but I haven't stopped to listen. I should have.

When I get into my flat, I collapse on the couch and close my eyes. My stomach grumbles, but getting up requires energy I don't have.

A tap on the door makes me open my eyes.

"Who is it?" I yell.

"Ginny."

Tiredness forgotten, I leap to my feet and get to the door.

"Hey." She smiles. "I wanted to check up on you."

I laugh. "I've got a killer headache still, but I'm okay."

"That's good. I stopped on the way and bought some fish and chips, if you're interested. If not, I'll take the leftovers home."

"Grease would probably help my head." I smile. "I thought you didn't eat gluten. There's got to be some in the fish batter."

Ginny shrugs. "It's not very much, and I could do with something different after the last few days."

I nod. "I know what you mean."

Stepping back, I usher her into the living room, and she opens the paper parcel on the coffee table while I grab a bottle of tomato sauce from the kitchen.

"Tough day at work?" she asks.

"It was okay once I got going. I was late. Mel came in and flicked water at me to wake me up at five."

Ginny laughs, sitting on the couch. "You were that sound asleep?"

"I was out to it."

She grins, shaking her head. "I guess you deserved it after the funeral."

"It wasn't an easy day. That's for sure. How about you? How was today?"

Her expression drops. "Up and down. I'm glad it's over."

"Me too." I pick up a piece of fish and bite the end off. The deliciousness that is beer batter and fresh fish greets me. The Copper Creek fish and chip shop makes sublime food. Everything's so fresh, and I eat far too much of it. Thankfully, I was blessed with good genes, though working out helps, too.

"This is so good." I look across, and Ginny's got a piece of fish of her own. "It's really going to hit the spot. A feed of this and some painkillers before bed, and that headache should clear up overnight." I smile. "Thank you for coming over. I meant it yesterday when I said I wanted to see more of you."

She bites down on her lower lip. "I'd really like that too. I've struggled with this, I really have. My head keeps telling me that I'm an idiot, but I think I saw a side of you yesterday that you don't let a lot of people see."

I look down to spy an onion ring at the top of the food, and smile.

Picking it up, I drop to the floor, kneeling before a bewildered Ginny. Her eyes are so full of confusion, but her lips twitch like she's amused. At least, I hope she is.

"Will you, Ginny Robinson, do me the honour of having dinner with me tomorrow night?"

She laughs, holding out her right hand, and I slide the onion ring on one of her fingers.

I swallow. "So, is that a yes?"

She grins. "Don't make me regret this. Yes."

My heart leaps at her words. From our conversation

yesterday, I knew she was interested but had her reservations. I have to keep working at it and showing her I mean it to break through. This is a start, though.

I've got my chance.

Now, to not screw it up.

***

OUR FIRST DATE is the following night.

I'm nervous like it's my very first date, and I'm pulling out all the stops to make this special.

I pick up Ginny from her place, letting out a low whistle when she appears in the doorway. Her long, auburn hair is hanging loose around her shoulders, and she's wearing a yellow dress. She looks like summer.

She's beautiful.

"Owen?"

"Sorry, what?" I realise I've been staring at her, and haven't moved from the same spot for I don't know how long. "It's just … you look gorgeous."

Her cheeks go pink, and I reach for her hand. "Ready?"

Ginny nods, and we walk to the car together.

"Where are we going?" she asks.

"To the cove. I have a place in mind."

There's a little bistro at the cove. It's small, quiet, and intimate. Perfect for a first date when all you really want is to be alone with someone.

When we get there, we're ushered to our table. I'm trying my best to impress Ginny tonight. Nothing will go wrong if I can help it.

With our food ordered, I smile at Ginny. "How was your day?"

Her happy expression falls. "It was okay."

"Only okay?"

She shrugs. "I'm just tired. It was a long one."

"I promise I won't keep you out too late."

Her eyes widen. "No, that's fine. It was just a long day at work. I'm glad I'm with you."

"I'm glad I'm with you, too. I've been thinking about this since yesterday."

She smiles. "Me too. I've been a bit nervous."

"Me too." I reach across the table and take her hand in mine. "I want tonight to be the beginning. Of what, I don't know yet, but I know I don't want it to be our only date."

Ginny nods, and my heart feels light. "That's what I want too."

Our chicken and salad arrives, and she lets go of my hand.

"Owen?" The waitress's gaze is on me.

I look up. *Shit.* "Uhh hi, Alicia."

This is not what I wanted to happen. I'd hoped that if I ran into anyone I'd slept with before, they wouldn't come near while I was obviously on a date. No such luck.

She smiles. "It's been a while. I was kinda hoping you'd call."

I flick a glance at Ginny. Her expression is tight, and I can't read it. Given how open she is, I hate it. "I'm on a date, but it was good to see you."

It's like Alicia suddenly sees Ginny, and she narrows her eyes. Over the years, I've been quite good at picking up the odd woman who said she wanted something casual, but after hooking up wanted more. Alicia was one of those.

"Oh. Sorry. Do you have my number?"

Are you for real? "I'm not sure, but like I said, I'm on a date right now."

She leans over, picking up a napkin from the table and scribbling a number on it. "Well, here you go if you need it."

"Thanks, but I'm sure I won't." Should I be even ruder to get rid of her and hope it doesn't upset Ginny? Here I am trying to make a good impression.

Alicia leans closer. "I always wished we could have had more than one night." She shifts her gaze to Ginny before moving it back to me.

"Well, clearly that's not going to happen. So, how about leaving us alone to enjoy our evening? I'm sure if Owen wants to, he'll call you."

I look across the table at Ginny. She casually takes a bite of her food, and smiles. She's so sweet and gentle, but the way she maintains her demeanour while telling Alicia to go away makes me hotter than the middle of summer.

Alicia straightens up and glares at Ginny. "I'm sure we'll talk again." She turns on her heel and walks across the room.

"That was amazing," I say.

"I'm guessing you didn't know whether or not to tell her to piss off." A smile crosses Ginny's lips.

"Your guess is right. I'm trying to impress you tonight, not look like a complete arsehole."

She shrugs. "It's okay. I knew all about this before I agreed to tonight. I'm not as fragile as you might think."

"I don't know what to think about you." I grin.

Ginny takes a sip of her drink. "I have two older brothers who still treat me like I'm made of china. The reality is that there have been things in my life that have made me tougher than I look. Plus, I had to be tough, having two older brothers."

"I know what you mean. My brothers and I still give each other shit all the time."

"I never would have guessed." Her eyes sparkle, and she radiates with happiness. What I thought would be a road bump in our night has turned out to be nothing.

But I'm not sure if that'll always be the case. There's still a lot for me to prove.

THE REST of the evening is quiet, and as much as I hate to say goodbye, I drive Ginny home. The whole way I'm replaying our interruption in my mind. *Could I have handled it better?*

I shoot a glance at her. She doesn't seem upset, but she is quiet.

What's going on with me? I never used to second guess myself.

Maybe wanting something more has made the difference.

When we get to her place, I get out of the car and open her door. Taking her hand, I close the car and we walk to her front door. "I'm sorry about our interruption."

Her eyes are sad, and I want anything to make them happy again.

For the first time in my life, I think I'm about to find out what it's like to have the person I'm keen on dump me.

She nods, letting out a sigh. "I knew what I was signing

up for when I said I'd go out with you. Your past is every-where in this town, Owen, and I either have to accept that or walk away." I close my eyes as she palms my cheek. "Just as well I like you enough to accept it. Doesn't mean I have to like it."

My eyes open to see her with the tiniest of smiles dancing on her lips. Thank God. She's going to give us a chance. "I couldn't stop what happened tonight, but I can promise you that while we're seeing each other, it'll only be you."

"That's all I want."

I've been aching to kiss her and now I take my chance. I lean in, claiming her mouth with mine. She responds, her lips parting, her tongue tentatively touching mine.

Yes. Her response gives me hope that things will work out, that what happened hasn't ruined things.

I could kiss her all night.

Instead, I remind myself that this is my one shot with her. I don't know where this is leading, but that last thing I want is to screw this up.

When our kiss finishes, I press my forehead to hers. "Call you tomorrow, Miss Robinson."

"I'll be waiting," she whispers.

With a brief brush of my lips against hers, I back off. "Get inside so I know you're safe."

She lets out a sigh, a broad smile on her face, and takes a step back, pushing open the door. "Good night, Owen."

"Good night."

I wait until the door is closed before taking a deep breath and pausing for a moment.

Despite our interruption, we seem to have survived the

night. Maybe I should feel sad that I'm going home alone, but instead I'm excited that she's still interested.

I can't wait to see her again.

7

<hr>

GINNY

MY STOMACH DROPS WHEN NATHAN WALKS INTO MY classroom the following day.

It's early. I like getting here well before the children arrive to make sure the lessons are prepared for the day, and the room set out for them. Often I'm the first one at school and the last one to leave.

Since I had Max in my class, my focus has been on those kids who need a little more help. Max wasn't getting what he needed before I got here, and there were a lot of people who wrote him off. Now, I couldn't be prouder of the progress he's made, and I know I've set him on the right track.

Which is what makes it so hard to think about leaving.

"Good morning, Ginny." This guy's so slimy, it's a miracle he doesn't leave a trail.

"Mr Webster."

He sits on the end of my desk and smiles. "I've told you before. Call me Nathan."

I nod, but say nothing.

"How are you feeling after the funeral? I couldn't help but notice you with Owen Campbell."

There's no way of telling where this is going, but it can't be good. I try my best not to be alone with Nathan. There are rumours about him being touchy-feely, and while I haven't experienced that, there's been plenty of innuendo.

My problem, is that he's been here for years, and I worry that when it comes down to it, the newer teacher on the block won't be believed. Not when there's no proof.

"I'm fine. It was very sad. And yes, I was with Owen. He needed comforting."

"You know, of course, that he was screwing Cara Mitchell. Along with so many other women in Copper Creek. Not the type you really want to associate with."

Anger builds in me. I've taken his comments about the way I dress, which is usually pretty conservative for school, but he's made me feel exposed. I've blown off the odd comment he's made about my body, usually in the form of a compliment, but not the type employers usually make to employees.

That's what drives me to think about leaving, despite my determination to help more kids here.

"Owen's a good man."

"I'm sure there are plenty of women to testify to that." His lips curl into a cruel smile.

"It's not really any of your business."

His expression hardens. "There's always a shoulder to cry on here when you need it."

"I won't." I'm usually so polite it takes everything in me to stop myself thanking him for his concern.

"Anyway, the other reason I'm here is that there's a conference coming up in Auckland about resources for special needs children. I thought with the way you took Max Parker under your wing that you might be interested in attending."

I'm staggered. The school has very little resources in that regard, and getting an opportunity to find ways to help would be wonderful. In the three years I've worked here, there's been nothing like this on offer.

"I'd be very interested. As you know, I think we can do a lot more."

He gives me a stiff nod. "I'll work on the details and will let you know." Standing, he takes a step closer. It's way too far into my personal comfort zone. "And remember, Ginny. I'm always here if you need comforting. Any time."

As he leaves, I find myself shaking and unsure of what that was.

But I do know I can't think about leaving town yet. Not if I have the opportunity to help more children.

Besides, Owen Campbell might just be another reason to stay.

8

OWEN

She's making me work for it, and I love it.

I don't know why this is different, as she's not the only woman who's ever been in my life who's done this. With the others who tried playing hard to get, I proved to them I could play harder by moving onto the next willing body. But Ginny's worth the wait.

Maybe it's because I never just stepped back and let nature take its course. I've always tried to take charge and steer things to what I always thought was the natural conclusion. Sex. There was never any "love them and leave them" because I didn't love.

Ginny's teaching me how.

We don't spend every evening together, but we are seeing each other at least three times a week. I want more, but I need to be patient for the first time in my life. It's surprisingly easy.

Seven weeks in, we still haven't had sex, but we are into

the heavy making out sessions. She leaves me hot and bothered, and I have to take care of myself, but I take great satisfaction in knowing she's suffering too.

I can sense it.

Like me, she wants to give into it, and the fight is getting harder. But I know more about her than any woman I have ever slept with. I long to see the face she makes when she comes, to hear the sounds she makes when she's being touched, to feel the rake of her fingernails down my spine.

All I want is her.

Seeing the result of that car accident brought a lot home to me. I don't want to die alone and unloved. I mean, I know my family love me, but finding one person to be with for the rest of my life doesn't seem too strange anymore. It's not just something everyone else does—I could do it too.

Is this love?

I don't know yet, but I do know I think about Ginny at night, and throughout the day. Mel teases me because I'm so easily distracted at times. It's just as well our ad attracted an assistant to help her. There are definitely times when I'm of no use.

Tammy appeared like a godsend. She's finished high school, but isn't going on to other studies. Plus, she loves baking. Between Mel and I, we'll teach her the job, and in the meantime, she's working in the store.

With a little more training, Tammy's presence will lighten the load, and I'll be able to spend more time with my girl without the constant tiredness during the week that's been the norm for so many years.

Thursday night is movie night, and Ginny and I are on

the couch in front of the television. Not that either of us are watching.

Ginny lies on top of me, her legs straddling my hips. Fully clothed, she grinds against me.

I stroke her breasts, and she gasps as I pinch her nipples through her clothing. This is about as far as we've gone, which leaves me aching, but I've slowly gotten to know her body and what she likes. By the time I get her naked, I'll be a master at Ginny Robinson.

"Damn, woman, you're gonna make a mess of me." I kiss up her neck as she leans over.

"It's payback for what you're doing to me," she whispers.

"What's that?" I take a gentle bite of her earlobe.

"Making it hard to hold back."

She sits up a little, and I meet her gaze. "Then don't."

"I should go." Her lips are pouty, still begging to be kissed. I could keep kissing her all night.

"Do you have to?"

She smiles. "I *should*."

"Does that mean there's a chance you'll stay?" I take her hand in mine. "We don't have to have sex."

Her eyes sparkle with warmth. "Is that ever going to work?"

"You mean because I can't keep my hands off you?"

She shakes her head. "I was thinking the reverse, actually. Maybe I'm the one with impulse issues."

"You can be as impulsive as you like with me." I grasp her chin and graze her lips with mine. "You know I have to be up at four, and it's after eleven now."

Ginny's mouth falls open. "It's that late?"

"Time flies when you're making out on the couch."

She laughs. "I really should go, then. Five hours' sleep isn't a lot."

"I'd sleep better with you."

Rolling her eyes, she pulls away. "Maybe next time."

I scan her expression. I'm happy with the pace we're going, and if she's not ready for sex, it doesn't matter to me. What concerns me is if she's holding back because of my past.

"Gin, you know it's only you, right? If that's what you're worried about."

She shifts her gaze to the ceiling. "I know. It's just—"

"You're scared I'm going to hurt you." My tone is flat, and I can't help it. I want things to be different for us, and it's been easy so far. I'm not interested in anyone but her, and that won't change when we do start a sexual relationship. How do I convince her of that?

"I'm sorry, Owen, but I am. Just a little." She drops her gaze back to me. "When we're together, it feels really good, but there are so many stories."

Shit. "Ginny, I can't stop the past, but I can promise you that I don't just want a fling. All these weeks I've tried to prove that this thing with us, it's different. Please stay. I just want you in my arms tonight. We don't need to have sex."

I mean every word. I know I need to earn her trust, and I'll do anything for it. She's so worth the effort.

"Okay."

"Really?"

She nods. "I love whatever this is that we have, and maybe it is different."

"I understand your hesitation if it helps. I'd be wary of me too."

Ginny's expression softens, and she gives me the tiniest of smiles. "You're doing everything right."

I cup her cheek. "I'm trying. And it's surprisingly easy, but you make it easy just by being you."

"I've already said yes. You know you don't have to talk me into staying, right?"

Laughing, I plant a kiss on her nose. "I'm not trying to impress you, but I do want to be honest with you."

"Just keep on being honest and we'll be fine."

I CAN'T BELIEVE I talked her into staying.

Taking her hand, I lead her to the bedroom where I drop my pants and pull my T-shirt over my head. I climb into bed dressed only in my briefs, and note Ginny's eyes on my chest.

She wriggles out of her jeans, dropping them to the floor, and I laugh as she reaches up inside her tank top and unhooks her bra.

"You're, uhh, pretty good at that."

"Years of practice while playing sport at school. When you're self-conscious, you learn ways to hide while changing."

I don't miss the lacy object being thrown on the floor, and she pulls back the bedcovers and slips into bed. "You played sport?"

"I played netball. My brothers played rugby, and I was the least sporty one out of the three of us, but it was something to do."

I reach for her waist and pull her toward me. "None of us

really played sport on a regular basis. Corey played rugby for a season before he started a brawl and got banned. He never bothered after that."

She laughs. "Are you close to your brothers? It seems like it."

I nod. "Yeah, we're all pretty close. Adam was away for years, but he's just slotted in like he used to. I was probably closer to Drew, as we shared a room until we moved here when I was twelve. Then we got a big enough house for us all to have space, but our relationships didn't change." I plant a kiss on the back of her neck. "What about you? Are you close to your family?"

"Very. I'm the only one who left Carlstown, though. My parents and brothers are still there."

"That close? I'd love to meet them."

She laughs. "I don't know if you want to do that."

Shrugging, I smile. "It can't be that bad. You know my family."

"My brothers can be a little overprotective."

Chuckling, I pull her in tighter, pressing my lips to the back of her head. "Then I'll just have to show them how much I respect their sister. If it's important to you, it's important to me."

"You know that's the perfect answer." She wriggles from my grasp and rolls onto her back.

This moment feels so natural, so right. I want it to happen again.

I want it to happen every night.

"I really want to make this work."

Her expression softens. "So do I."

I lick my lips. "As much as I want you—and I do, there's

no doubt about that—I respect what you're doing. You need to learn to trust me, and I need to gain that trust. I'll do whatever it takes."

She nods, and I bend my head to press my lips to hers. After all these years, it's like coming home being with Ginny, and I don't want the feeling to ever end.

When I close my eyes, she's in my arms, and all is right in my world.

I GROAN as the alarm beeps, and reach behind me, slapping the stop button.

Ginny's moved in the night, and she rolls over to face me.

"Sorry," I murmur, leaning to place a kiss on her forehead. "What time do you need to get up?"

"Around seven would be good. It'll give me enough time to get home and change. One of my students will notice I'm wearing yesterday's clothing, knowing my luck."

I chuckle and reach for the clock. "The alarm's set." I reach over and stroke her cheek. "Thank you for staying."

Giving her a final kiss, I fling my legs over the side of the bed and stand. I grab a pair of jeans and a T-shirt from my drawers and pull them on.

"Owen?" Her voice is husky, and such a big part of me wants to stay with her until she has to leave for the day.

"Yes?"

"You don't work Saturdays, right?"

"Nope. The bakery's Mel's baby then."

"Want me to stay tonight, too? Maybe we can do more than sleep."

I lean over. The room is dark, but not so dark I can't make out her features. "Is that you propositioning me, Miss Robinson?"

"You make me sound like the naughty school teacher."

I run my tongue across the seam of her lips before giving her a tender kiss. "Maybe that's what I'm hoping for."

She laughs, propping herself up to reach over and slap me on the arse. "We'll see. Get to work. Your town needs bread."

"Yes, boss."

Giving her a final peck, I head out the door with a smile on my face.

I've won her trust.

IT's the longest eleven hours of my life.

Knowing what's waiting for me tonight, or rather, who, leaves me on edge the entire day.

Usually, I close the bakery at five, but by four, I've had enough.

"Go home, you two. I'm shutting up for the day."

Both Mel and Tammy look at me with open mouths. I never close early.

"Are you feeling alright?" Mel asks.

"I'm fine. I've just got things on tonight, and I need to focus."

"Are those things about five-foot-six, gorgeous, and brunette?"

I laugh. "Something like that."

"I'd close up early too if I had her to focus on."

Tammy's still not used to the way Mel and I speak to each other, and she stands in the corner, her cheeks glowing red.

"Well, this one's all mine, so keep your eyes to yourself." I chuckle.

"Fair enough. I'm going to assume we'll still be paid for the last hour."

"As if I'd do anything different. See you ladies tomorrow."

I'm closing the door when Corey and Adam appear.

At the sight of the box of beer in Corey's hand, I roll my eyes. Of all nights, this is not going to be a boozy one for me. "Having a few drinks?"

He grins. "We thought we'd come and bug you for a while."

I fix my gaze on Adam. "What about you? Don't you have dinner at home or something?"

"Corey came around to our place, and we were getting under Lily's feet. She told us to come and see you for a couple of hours."

Chuckling, I nod. "Fair enough. Bring the beers in. Most of them must be for me, given I'm the one not driving."

When we get to the living room, I collapse on the couch. Adam and Corey sit in the recliners, and Corey opens the box, handing out the beers. If they don't leave before Ginny gets here, I'll kick them out, but for the moment, Adam and Corey are a welcome distraction.

"So how are things going with you and Ginny?" Adam asks.

"Why?"

He grins. "You know why. Because you've been seeing her since Drew's wedding, and that's not like you."

I nod. "Yes, we are still seeing each other. And I hope it continues. Ginny's awesome."

"Awesome." Corey snorts. "How old are you? Twelve?"

"Fine. She's a beautiful, intelligent, gentle, caring woman. Is that enough for you?"

Corey nods. "It sounds more grown-up. And what Adam said. Not like you."

"Maybe it's time for me to grow up." I push myself to sit.

Adam raises his beer bottle, and I clink mine to it. "Here's to growing up," he says. "It is kinda awesome."

Nodding toward him, I smile. "Well, who would have thought things would end up like this for you? Settled down with Lily and your kids. Took a while, but it must feel good."

"Best feeling ever."

That's the life what I want. Settled.

I lick my lips. "Ginny stayed over for the first time last night."

"No way," Corey said. "Drew's wedding was weeks ago."

"We've been taking things slowly. You guys should be proud of me because Ginny and I haven't had sex yet."

"So, let me get this straight. You spent the entire night with a woman in your bed, and you didn't have sex? That has to be a first." Corey chuckles.

"I'd just like to point out that she's the first woman I've had in *my* bed."

Adam leans forward. "Really?"

I shrug. "I always had this theory that it was easier to move on if I was the one leaving."

Corey shakes his head. "I had no idea you were that sad. But I guess it makes sense."

I raise my middle finger at him. "It's worked for a really long time."

"Can I ask you something?" He takes a sip of his beer.

"What?"

"Why her? I mean, I don't really know her, so I can't judge for myself, but why after all this time is this one different?"

I let out a loud puff of breath. "She cares. I'm not saying no one else ever has, but with Ginny, it's so deep. When I've needed her, she's been there, and I don't think she's had any expectations."

"So, like a babysitter?"

I laugh. "Damn it, Corey. I can't explain it. With Cara's death, it's really got me thinking about what a short time we have and how much I might have missed out on. Ginny just gets me. It feels right."

His lips quirk. "Good for you."

"What happened with you and that blonde from Drew's wedding? Are you ever going to tell us? Are you seeing her again?" Adam asks Corey.

Corey rolls his eyes. "We went back to her motel room, with her telling me the whole way what she wanted me to do to her. It was hot as fuck until she literally fell asleep as soon as she fell into bed."

I roar with laughter. "So what did you do?"

"I was too drunk to go anywhere else, so I grabbed a pillow and slept on the couch."

The mental image is hilarious. Corey's six-foot-some-thing-ridiculous, and I know how small the couches are in that motel.

Adam laughs. "Dude. Surely it would have been easier to sleep on the floor?"

"I was drunk. It made sense at the time. My back hurt like a bitch in the morning."

Corey shifts his gaze to me. "I don't know what I'm gonna do if you settle down. That just puts more pressure on me."

"As if anyone's ever pressured you into anything." I laugh. "How are things going with the cops on your land?"

Corey currently has the police surveying his neighbours from halfway down his property. It's a mutual arrangement made after the shit Ash Harris pulled on Drew's wife, Hayley, and I know it's gone on far longer than Corey would have liked.

The smile disappears from his face. "All I know is that they're there for the long haul." He lets out a breath. "That truck that hit Cara and Ryan. Guess where it was coming from?"

"The mountain?"

"Apparently it drove up to those gates, dropped off whatever was inside, and left again. The driver was going way too fast, Owen. They never stood a chance."

I place my beer on the coffee table and bury my head in my hands. "So, let me get this straight. While the police take their sweet time over all this, that lot have managed to ruin more lives?"

"Dude. I'm sorry. I thought you should know. The undercover cops are still relatively new in the community, and they're not in deep enough. But whatever was in that truck is the key. They're sure of it."

"Do they have any more clues?"

He shakes his head, gripping my shoulder. "If they do, they're not telling me. That truck driver had a wife and kids too, so it wasn't just Cara and Ryan's girl left behind. I mean, was he speeding to get home, or just to get away from whatever he'd delivered? How bad is all this?"

Ava.

She still occupies my thoughts. I made a very angry phone call to Graham Taylor the morning after the funeral to request an update on Ava and complain about what happened that day. That poor kid. I've never dealt with anything like that before in my time as a volunteer fireman, and I hope to God I never have to again.

"They have to get to the bottom of all of this," I growl.

"They will. I have to be patient because those lumbering oafs think they're being quiet where they're camped out in the little hut they've built, but there's no wildlife within half a freaking kilometre of my place now. But there's no way I'm giving up, or blocking them from doing what they have to do because Ash tried to hurt Hayley." He sighs. "That shit's unforgivable. I want Ash Harris locked away for a very, very long time."

I nod.

It's the least that bastard deserves.

9

GINNY

Nathan Webster still gives me the creeps.

There are rumours about him. Rumours that no one will confirm, but I'm pretty sure people just don't want to rock the boat in a small town with limited employment options.

Nathan eyes me from the other side of the staffroom. The way he casts his gaze over me leaves me with a stomach ache.

I'm almost thankful when Becky walks toward me.

"Can I talk to you?"

I suck a breath in. I've been waiting for this moment as I knew it would become public knowledge Owen and I were seeing each other. I'm surprised she's waited this long to say something. We've already discussed his past with Becky, my co-worker, but until now she's not said anything about Owen and me. Now it seems that's about to change. "Sure."

She licks her lips as she sits beside me, obviously trying to choose her words wisely. "It's about you and Owen Campbell."

I nod. "I thought it might be."

Her eyes widen, as if it's a surprise that I already know what she wants. "I don't want to interfere, but I do have some experience when it comes to him."

It takes everything in me to stop an eye roll. I'm well aware of Becky's past with Owen, both that they screwed around, and that she practically stalked him afterward. That is from my own personal observation too, and not because of anything he'd told me. "I know you do, but Owen and I are seeing each other and we're happy."

"You'll be happy until he moves onto the next one."

For a second, I close my eyes. I can't pretend I haven't thought about this, but it's been nearly two months, and Owen's doing everything right. He hasn't given me any reason not to trust him, even when I feel like I'm looking for one. "He's changed, Becky. I know you don't believe it, but I do."

"Leopards never change their spots." She sighs. "Look. I'm not warning you because I have any feelings left where he's concerned, but I like you, and I don't want to see you hurt."

"I've got no reason to think he's going to hurt me." I let out a loud breath in exasperation. "He's been through a lot, and he's working out what's important." My heart sings at the thought of his dedication to me so far. If it was just about sex, I'm sure he would have given up weeks ago. I don't think he's seriously romanced a woman before, but Owen's bending over backwards to get me to fall in love with him. Not that he's really had to try hard. I do love him. Just the thought warms my heart.

"Just don't let him break your heart in the process. Trust

me, Ginny, it'll be a matter of time before he moves onto the next one and leaves you in his wake. It's what he does."

I swallow hard. "Not this time."

In that moment, I know I'm lost. Lost in love with Owen, and way past the point of no return. He's been so patient and sweet, never putting any pressure on me to have sex with him, even though I seem to keep hearing from everyone else from everyone else that's all he wants. And yet, I know how much he wants me.

I want him, too.

10

OWEN

AFTER AN HOUR, COREY AND ADAM HEAD BACK TO ADAM'S for dinner. Adam invites me, but I decline the offer because nothing is getting in the way of me spending time with my girl. Especially not tonight.

Tonight is all about Ginny and me.

I can't remember a time when I was this nervous. I've skated through most of my life with casual flings, but this woman means so much more to me, and I want this night to be special.

When the knock on the door comes, I have to calm myself. I'm going to worship her like the goddess she is. I'm going to show her just how much she means to me.

Because I know she will have heard otherwise.

The thought of that punches me in the gut. When I decided never to settle down it was for what I thought were all the right reasons. But putting everything that's happened in perspective lately, what a stupid decision that was.

"Hey." Her smile illuminates the room, and there's something behind it I haven't seen before.

"Hi, beautiful." I lean over and give her a tender kiss, lingering on the lips I've been missing since this morning. "I've made dinner." She scans my face, and I smile. "What?"

"I want you to know that someone told me today that I'd be hurt when you move on."

My heart sinks. "Becky, by any chance?"

"How'd you guess?" A smile still plays on her lips, and she doesn't sound upset. "I told her this was different, and that you'd changed. She didn't believe me."

"As long as you know. Everything that's happened lately has taught me a lot about myself. She doesn't know that."

"But I do. I've seen it."

My heart leaps at her faith in me. I grab hold of her hand. "Let's go and eat. I made pasta."

Her eyebrows twitch. "I haven't had pasta in forever."

"It's even gluten-free. I made it fresh myself. The things I do for my girl."

She laughs. "You spoil me."

"You're worth the effort. Mind you, I'm not exactly sure how it's going to taste, so be prepared for anything."

As I take a step toward the kitchen, Ginny grabs my hand. "I don't care what anyone says, Owen. I know your heart."

"You probably know it better than anyone else." I squeeze her hand before continuing to the kitchen.

Her faith in me leaves me feeling better than anything has in a long time.

I'M NOT TOO sure about my pasta attempt. I frown as I chew my way through it. Ginny doesn't complain once.

I'm a baker, not a chef.

Afterward, I clean away the dishes, and she makes herself comfortable on the couch. Nerves chew at my stomach. This is insane.

She smiles as I enter the room. That smile lights up my whole world.

"Sorry for dinner."

Ginny laughs. "What do you mean? It was lovely."

I shrug as I sit beside her. "I'm not sure if lovely's the right word."

"It was made by you. That's what makes it special."

I reach for her face, locking my fingers in her hair and pulling her closer. "You're special."

My mouth meets hers and I close my eyes as the familiarity of her kiss floods my system. I never thought I'd feel this way, and it's corny as hell, but Ginny completes me. She's like the other half of my soul.

We were just meant to be. I'm sure of it. Everything in my life has led me to her, and I'm not about to ignore that.

"Are you ready for bed?" I ask.

"Yes," she whispers, and every nerve in my body stands to attention.

"Are you sure? We don't have to. There's no rush." I can't believe I'm talking myself out of sex. That is definitely not like me.

"It's time, Owen. I'm not going to make myself wait any longer."

My heart catches alight at her words. These past few

months, while I've been desperately wanting to do more than just kiss her, the last thing I wanted was to apply any pressure. The thought of sinking into her makes my body ache. And now she wants me.

For the first time in my adult life, I feel woefully inadequate and wonder if I can fulfil her needs. Maybe the anticipation of this has played with my head a little too much.

"What's brought this on?" I ask.

"I just want to be with you."

Wrapping my arms around her waist, I look into her eyes. "You're with me regardless. I only want to take the next step if you're completely ready. And yeah, I know this might seem weird coming from me, but I want this thing to work with you."

"It will." Her smile brightens the room, and any more thoughts of delay leave my brain.

She wants me. I want her.

There's simply nothing else left.

***

SHE SHIVERS as I unzip her dress and run my index finger down her spine.

This is like getting the best Christmas present ever, and the anticipation is killing me.

Turning to face me, Ginny's gaze sweeps over my face as she reaches for the hem of my T-shirt.

I'm as nervous as a teenage boy on a first date.

As she throws my shirt on the floor, I pull her into my arms.

"Owen," she whispers.

I raise my hands to her shoulders and slide the sleeves of her dress down her arms.

"You're so beautiful," I say.

Her dress drops to the floor, and this time she's got nowhere to hide as I unclip her bra.

Our lips brush, and I catch a glimpse of her perky breasts before she presses them against my chest. The feel of her skin against mine is divine, and I close my eyes as I drop kisses down her neck.

I groan at the feeling of her hands on the waistband of my jeans. Her breathing accelerates as she flips the button and unzips me.

"I need you," she says.

Pushing my jeans down, I kick them off, laughing softly as her hands are already on the elastic of my boxers.

"Impatient?" I ask.

"Very."

Ginny in her underwear was hot. Ginny naked is spectacular.

Nothing's coming between us tonight.

Her eyes settle on my cock as she removes my last piece of clothing, and I smile. I'm already hard from the extensive making out session on the couch. This time I don't have to deal with it myself, which only makes me harder.

Tonight, I'll be with her.

She sucks in a breath as I climb into bed beside her, running my fingers from her neck, and down the side of her body. I kiss my way from her shoulder to her breast, taking the delicate pink nipple into my mouth and caressing it with my tongue. She shivers.

"You okay?" I ask.

"Just a bit nervous. I don't know why."

I grin. "Anticipation? It's the same for me. I want this to be perfect for you so badly."

"What about you?"

Pushing myself up, I lose myself in her lips for a moment. She's so warm and familiar, but makes my heart race when I kiss her. "Being with you makes this perfect," I whisper.

"Owen."

I bend my neck and return my attention to her breasts. This is one night when I'm not going to be in any rush. One night when I'm not running away.

What I always thought would be the hardest thing of all is made simple because I'm in love. And as strange a feeling as that is for me, I revel in it.

Ginny sighs, but it's a contented sigh, and she scrapes her nails over my scalp. The gentle gesture drives me on. I want her to feel everything when she's with me, just as I feel everything right now.

I take my time, pressing kisses down her torso until I'm between her legs. When I look up and into her eyes, they're full of emotion, and I know she's feeling this as much as I am. There's something special between us. There's no denying that.

Her breath catches, and I smile. She squirms before I make contact with her clit, and her moans are barely audible when I do. But I hear them. I notice everything about her.

I play her with my tongue, her moans growing louder. Straightening up, I insert two fingers inside her. Her chest rises and falls rapidly, her breath laboured as I press as deep as I can.

"Owen," she cries as I stroke her clit with my thumb. I'm giving it everything I've got. I'm never going to give her a reason to regret giving me a chance. Her eyelids flutter as she comes. She's relaxed and as ready for me as I am for her.

I lean over and kiss her. Her body shivers underneath mine, and she grips my bicep as I pull a foil package from the box on the bedside cabinet.

I unwrap it and roll the condom on, maintaining eye contact with her. If I'm right, her nerves are gone. Written all over her face is the adoration we share for one another.

I love Ginny.

The thought overwhelms me, and makes me want her even more. Never did I think I'd feel this way, to want and need someone so much it's filled my heart with more love than I can handle.

I've held nothing back from her so far, and I won't hold back from this either.

"Are you okay?" A smile plays on her lips.

"I hope you know how much I love you."

There. The words are said, and her smile widens.

"I love you too." She takes a deep breath as I push into her. Any thoughts of anything else but Ginny are gone as we join for the first time. If this is what sex is like when you love someone, I want more. More with her.

Moving slowly, I keep kissing her. She's all around me, and I don't want to lose this feeling.

In a moment of clarity, I understand Drew and Hayley, Adam and Lily. If there was ever anyone for me, it's Ginny, and the only regret I have is that it's taken me so long to find her.

Now I have her, there's no way I'll do anything to risk this.

She's mine.

Tension builds in my body. It's not a new sensation, but it's somehow different this time. Maybe it's because I've just told her how I feel, and I know she feels the same way. She's everything I never knew I wanted.

And I want this all of the time.

I pick up the pace. She moans at first, and as I drive in deeper, her expression grows more serious. "Are you okay?"

Ginny takes a deep breath. "You're so deep."

"Want me to ease up a bit?"

She nods.

I slow again, and focus on kissing her. Whatever it takes to make her happy, I'll do it.

"That feels good," she says.

Our gazes lock. She fights the urge to close her eyes, I can see it. And I lose myself in the moment, warmth washing over me as I come. "God, Ginny."

Confusion crosses her face. "What?"

"Being with you. It's everything."

Tears well in her eyes.

I kiss her, rolling to her side and pulling her with me. Her skin's so soft beneath my hands as I stroke her back and thighs. All I want is my hands on her, and she's not complaining. The smallest of contented sighs catches in her throat, and it bewitches me.

One night of this will never be enough.

"No regrets?" I ask.

She shakes her head.

"Me either. And I want more. I know you want to move slowly, and I'll do whatever it takes to make you happy. You're all I want."

Ginny nestles in closer, draping her arm across my chest. I grasp her hand and press it to my lips.

I don't ever want to let her go.

11

DREW

Keeping Hayley's pregnancy a secret is tough.

I understand her reasons, but it takes everything in me not to yell it from the rooftops every single day.

The hard part has been watching her struggle with morning sickness, though it's passing now.

As we reach the end of the first trimester, she glows, and I'm more in love with her than ever. She's taken a job with a group of independent midwives, and her workload is a lot lighter these days, which leaves me relieved. It'd be tough doing this with the way she used to run around in Copper Creek.

It's time for our first scan. After a rough few weeks, Hayley chose a midwife and everything seems well. Now we get to take a look at our baby, and I can see for myself how things are going.

I grip her hand. "Ready?"

She smiles and nods.

The gel's smeared over her stomach. There's already a small bump there. I kiss it every time we make love, knowing my child's inside her. I always wanted a big family, and that we've started fills me with more joy than I can say.

That it's with Hayley only makes it better.

Jan, the technician, runs the transducer across Hayley's skin before settling in one place. The image clears, and there's our active, kicking baby. At a glance, it's perfectly formed and very much alive.

And then I spot it.

"Hayley?"

She squeezes my hand. "Yes?"

I look closer. "Is that …?"

Jan looks up. "You see that too?"

I nod. "One appears to be hiding behind the other, but that looks like twins to me."

All the colour in Hayley's face disappears. "Really?"

"It would explain the more severe morning sickness. Even if you'd had a scan earlier, we might not have picked it up. We've got a shy one, babe."

She laughs. "I know you wanted a big family, but twins?"

I chuckle. "It'll have to be confirmed, but if anyone asked me, I'd say either we have one baby with four legs, or there are two babies."

"Let's see if we can pick up both heartbeats," Jan says.

She turns the volume up, and the rapid beat fills the room. I close my eyes, and nod. "The other one's faint, but it's there."

As Jan moves the transducer around, and the second beat grows in volume.

"There you are," she says.

I open my eyes at Hayley's gasp. Sure enough, we're not having one baby. There are two.

Hayley's grip tightens, and I lean over, giving her a tender kiss. "We're in for a ride." I chuckle.

"Two babies. How are we going to cope with two babies?" she asks.

"We'll be fine. I'm in shock, but I'm sure we'll be fine."

She laughs. "You might be. I don't know how I'm gonna do."

I shift my gaze to her. "It'll be good, babe. We'll do it together."

"Are you going to give birth?"

"If I could, I would. I'd take the pain over you dealing with it."

Hayley shoots me a look that leaves me wanting to drag her out of here and take her home to bed. Instead, I refocus on the ultrasound. We're at fourteen weeks, and the anatomy scan will come later, but our babies really do look perfect.

Our babies.

"So I guess this means we can start telling people?" I ask.

Hayley grins. "I guess it does. I'll call my parents when we get home."

"Fancy a road trip? I want to see everyone's reactions in person."

"When?"

"Let's go and see your mum and dad on Saturday, stay the night, and then see my family on Sunday. Maybe take Monday off to rest up."

She laughs. "That's a lot of travelling."

"Yeah, but can you imagine how excited our parents will

be? Your mum is going to flip out." I plant a kiss on her forehead.

Everything's perfect.

WE GET HOME, and Hayley heads straight to the couch.

She's been quiet in the car, and I know she's worried. If I could wrap her in bubble wrap for the next six months, I would. I'm worried too.

"How are we going to cope?" I can see the concern in her eyes.

I smile, sitting beside her and pulling her into my arms. "We'll get there. It's not going to be easy, but you know I'll be with you every step of the way."

"I know. It's just …"

She doesn't need to finish that sentence. I know her well enough to know what she's thinking.

"Our plans don't need to change. You'll be on maternity leave and decide what you want to do. And I'll back you the whole way, whether you want to go back to work or not. We can live on my salary."

Her shoulders slump. "I know. It was just going to be a lot easier with one baby."

"It could have been worse. At least there are only two."

She laughs, leaning her head against mine. "I guess you're right."

"Of course I am. I'm always right. That's what husbands are for."

Hayley lets out a loud sigh. "I guess I should have ordered one without a big ego."

"It's why you love me. Isn't it?" I rub her back. "It's not just my ego that's big either."

She shakes her head. "You never fail to make me laugh."

"Constant entertainment. That's me. Isn't that how we ended up in this position?"

Hayley pulls away, looking at me with so much love it takes my breath away. "I love you."

"Love you too, princess. More than anything."

She grabs one of my hands, pressing it to her stomach. "I don't know about anything."

"Okay. Well, maybe those two have a bit of my heart, but their mother's the best thing that ever happened to me."

"Right back at you, Campbell."

I could worry more about multiple pregnancies and increased risk, and given my occupation, maybe I should, but right now I'm on cloud nine knowing that in a few months we'll have two beautiful babies.

I've got everything I ever wanted.

12

OWEN

It's been nine weeks since Cara died.

Nine weeks since I met Ginny.

Graham has passed on my concerns about Ava's care, but I've heard nothing. Meanwhile, the butchery stands closed, though I've heard they've tempted a butcher from Carlstown to rent the place. Before long, things will be back to being as normal as they've ever been around here.

I've got eyes for no one but Ginny. My green-eyed girl has me running around in circles, and I've never been happier.

I'm not sure if it's because I've had to face the idea of my mortality that's got me so settled with her, or if it's just that she's such a good person. She's big-hearted, and more loving than most people I know.

She's spent two nights at my place this week, and even though I want her with me every night, we're taking things slow.

It's Friday, and I get my only real sleep-in of the week. I've decided to have a long weekend, and Mel has the new assistant to help her. If she really needs me, she knows where to find me. But today, all the sleep is mine.

Until the knock on my door.

I roll over, and open one eye to see the alarm clock. It's 8:35 a.m. And whoever is interrupting my sleep had better have a good reason for it.

Tugging on some trackpants and a T-shirt, I drag myself to the back door. It's Marie, the social worker who picked Ava up that fateful day.

What the hell is she doing at my house?

"Hi."

"Hi, Owen." Her tone is soft, as if she has some bad news for me. What the hell else can there be?

"If you're here because I complained about the day of Cara and Ryan's funeral, it's a bit early in the morning. And late. That was two months ago."

She nods. There's no colour in her cheeks. "Can I come in?"

"Uhh, sure."

She follows me into the living room, and I point at the couch.

"What's this all about?"

Marie licks her lips. "Cara and Ryan left everything in a bit of a mess. There's been a lot of sifting through documents and trying to get to the bottom of everything. Anyway, I'm here about Ava."

"What about her?" I sit in a recliner opposite, but lean forward.

"There's no easy way to say this, Owen." She takes a deep breath. "But you're her father."

I blink in rapid succession.. "I'm her what?"

"Cara and Ryan had a lawyer who handled a lot of their business stuff. But she had a will lodged with another lawyer, and she named you as Ava's real father and as the girl's legal guardian. You should get your lawyer to go through the court and get a parenting order, and if I were you I'd get a DNA test done to change her birth certificate …"

My chest tightens as my mind whirls, and I stop hearing what she's saying. "Cara's family …"

"That little girl has no family. Just you." Marie hands me an envelope. "It's all in here. Cara's lawyer will also be in touch. With her naming you legal guardian, I thought it best to bring her here straight away."

"Don't you have to vet me too?"

She gives me a small smile. "Well, Cara naming you as testamentary guardian gives you automatic guardianship of Ava. As well as that, you had a full police background check when you joined the volunteer fire brigade."

I shake my head. "I can't believe this. Surely she would have said something."

"Surely you suspected?"

I shrug. "When it was over, she told me she and Ryan were back together and that they'd been blessed. I was happy for her."

"Ava needs you, Owen." Marie shifts her gaze to the floor. "She's been so unsettled, and she was onto her fifth family when I got the news. I can try and find something more permanent, but it won't be close."

"Five families? In two months?"

She nods. "She needs you."

If Ava really is my child, I need to do something, but my feet are lead and I can't work out how to use them. For the first time in my life, I really don't know what to do.

"Owen?"

I nod, pushing myself to stand. "I'm not letting her go to another family. Not when she has one here."

Her brows knit. "Are you sure?"

It's going to be hard. I've never planned a family. I've never planned anything like this.

But I can't let Ava go on the way she has been. I'm not ready, I'm scared, but I think of Cara and although it's upsetting she didn't tell me I was Ava's father when she was still alive, she ultimately did the right thing making a will that told the truth.

"If I'm her father, I'd be a shitty one if I let her go somewhere else."

She nods. "I'm so sorry I didn't know all those weeks ago, Owen."

"Yeah, me too."

"Where is she?"

I STOP when I see her. *Am I the man for this job?*

Ava's sitting on a chair on the back deck with another social worker. Her feet swing and her head is bowed, her long blonde hair hanging down. This poor kid has probably been to hell and back, and here I am, hesitating.

"Hey Ava." My voice cracks, and she raises her face to look at me.

I never paid attention to Cara's kid, but now my genes scream back at me when I see her. Maybe it's because I've had the benefit of seeing Max and Rose from an early age, but from what I can see, there's a family resemblance.

"You're going to come and live with me. Is that okay?"

The poor girl looks terrified, but I know it's not personal. She's been shipped from pillar to post the past couple of weeks. I need to give her some stability.

"So you know what? Remember the gingerbread men I gave you before?"

She nods, her eyes widening.

"Maybe we can make a special one just for you."

If baking for Ava is what gets through to her, what helps ease her into whatever new life is in store for her, I'll do it. It's all I know how to do.

She gives me a small smile.

I have a two-bedroom flat. At least I can give her a room of her own, and we can pretty it up for her.

My stomach sinks. What's Ginny going to think? I've finally found someone I might just want to settle down with, and this happens. She's already struggling with my history as a playboy, and now I have a daughter with someone from that past.

"Her things are in the suitcase."

I raise my gaze and frown at the small case beside her.

"That's it? What about all her toys?"

Ava bursts into tears, and I feel useless.

"We packed as much as we could. There'll be a lawyer in touch with you in the next few days. There'll be an inheritance for her from the estate. I'm not sure about the exact details. Cara's lawyer will have all of the information."

"As much as you could," I mutter.

She places her hand on my shoulder. "I'm sorry, Owen. We didn't have a lot to work with."

Shrugging her off, I reach for Ava's hand. At least she trusts me enough to take it.

"We can help settle her in."

I turn back to Marie. "What you can do is piss off. I'll take it from here."

To her credit, she doesn't even blink, but she nods. "I'll be in touch."

"Please don't."

I pick up the case, and lead Ava into the house, dropping her bag on the living room floor.

"Come on." I lead her out through the bakery kitchen and to the front of the shop. Mel looks up at me, confusion on her face, and nods toward Ava.

"Long story."

I take Ava around to the display cabinet that contains the gingerbread men. "There you go, sweetheart. Pick whichever one you want."

Her eyes are so big as I settle her on my hip and slide the glass cabinet open, and she slowly reaches her hand out to take one. I smile. "It's okay."

I need to go through her bag. What does she have in there? Just clothing? Has she got a toothbrush, pyjamas, everything else she actually needs? There's so much to think about.

I set Ava down to eat her biscuit.

"Owen? Why is the Mitchell kid here?" Mel mutters.

"Because she's my daughter."

Now her eyes widen as she stares at me. "Serious?"

"Apparently so. She's my responsibility."

Her face falls. "That poor child."

"Thanks."

She laughs. "Oh, no, not that you're her dad. I'm glad about that. Everything she must have been through, and she gets to live with someone who'll take care of her and who makes delicious baked goods."

Shaking my head, I look down at Ava. There are crumbs all over the floor, which would normally drive me bonkers, but I couldn't bring myself to be angry with her if I tried. While I'm still trying to come to terms with the news I'm a father, it angers me that she hasn't had the ground under her feet during the last few months. I might not know how to feel, but at least she'll have stability with me.

"Okay, kiddo. Let's go sort out this bedroom for you."

The least I can do is to try and make this as easy for her as possible.

She follows me back into the flat, and I grab her bag on the way through.

The room smells a bit musty. It's my spare room, with a double bed it in, and it's not been used much, but I pull the curtains and open the window to let some fresh air in.

Ava wrinkles her nose.

"It's okay. By the time you go to bed, it won't smell so funky. I don't use this room much, but we'll make it better for you."

I pull open a drawer in the dressing table, and pick up her suitcase.

There's fuck all in it.

I fume as I pluck out three tops and two pairs of leggings. There's one pair of pyjamas and a spare pair of socks, but that's it. The only other thing in the case is a tattered teddy-bear.

Ava grabs the bear from my hands and holds it tight, giving me a defiant look as if she thinks I'm going to take it off her.

I ruffle her hair. "Is that your friend?"

She nods.

"Well, there are enough things here to get us started. Looks like we'll have to do some shopping." I smile. "Have you had anything else to eat this morning?"

Ava shakes her head.

"How about I make some toast and hot chocolate? You already had the cookie." I grin. There's so much of Cara in there, but the more I look closely at Ava, the more I see me. Did Ryan ever see it? If they were that desperate, did he even care?

"Yes, please."

I smile at the sound of her voice. "I might even have some marshmallows I can add to the hot chocolate."

Her eyes widen. I'll have to learn not to go overboard with sweet things, and I'm going to have to make sure I buckle down on her looking after her teeth.

Wait. Is that a dad thing to think?

"Come here." I pat the bed, and she climbs up beside me.

I don't really know what to say, but I know I need to say something.

"Do you know why you're here?"

Ava shakes her head.

I let out a breath. "I don't really know how to explain this, but I'm your other dad. So you get to stay here now."

Her blonde eyebrows knit. "Jackie said I don't have a daddy anymore."

Jackie. I still bristle at the way she knocked back my gift to Ava on the day of the funeral.

"Well, Jackie's wrong about a lot of things. You don't have to call me Dad. I know that'll be a bit weird. Owen will do." I smile. "You've got a whole family to meet." *And then there's my girlfriend who might just decide this is too much to handle.*

I can't think about that, won't think about it. Right now I need to sort out everything Ava needs and put some ground beneath her feet.

But for now, I need breakfast, and I'm sure Ava does too.

She wolfs down four pieces of toast like they don't even touch her sides, and I frown. At least she won't have to worry about food here.

This is so weird.

How do I do this? And what do I do now?

I SPEND the rest of the day around the house, unsure of what to do next.

Ginny's not responding to texts, and while we didn't have plans for tonight, I need her with me. I need to tell her.

Ava falls asleep straight after dinner. Today would have been a long day, and for a moment, I stare at her, curled up on the floor, and I have no idea what to do next.

I never thought I was destined to have a stable relationship, let alone one with a kid. Adam and Lily know way more about this stuff than I do. Maybe tomorrow I'll take her over there and ask for help.

My phone buzzes.

Sorry I didn't reply earlier. I've been in bed with a headache most of the day. It's clear now.

Ginny. What's she going to think?

I'm sorry to hear that. Want to come over and stay the night? If she still wants to be with me after she hears my news.

You could come here if you want.

I pick up the sleeping child on the floor and carry her to bed, thankful that I got it right and had her in her pyjamas before dinner.

Placing her gently in on the mattress, I pull up the duvet. The room smells fresh now, and I close the window and pull the curtains before going back out to the living room.

I need you to come here because I have something important I want to talk to you about.

Is everything okay?

It will be when you're here.

Be there in ten.

My eyes wander to the hallway. Ava's in a strange bed in a strange house, and maybe it'd be a good idea to leave the hall light on.

If she's going to be here permanently, I'll have to make changes to so many things.

What do I do with her during the day when I'm working? I haven't even thought about that. There's a day care not far from here. Maybe I can look into that.

There are so many things to think about.

But I don't regret that she's here. Five homes in nine weeks.

I sit on the couch and close my eyes. Nine weeks ago, I was happy and celebrating my brother's wedding. Drew and

Hayley went through their rough times, but they came out stronger on the other side.

Ginny and I are so new and fragile. It's taken those nine weeks to build trust with her, and just when we get there …

I open my eyes and sigh, picking up the remote control. I need something to keep focused on while I wait. The irony of something this big happening just when I think I've found the girl I might want to settle down with isn't lost on me.

There's a soft knock on the door, and I catch my breath before rising to open it.

She's there, all green eyes and kind smile, her raised eyebrows displaying her curiosity.

I don't say anything. I pull her into my arms and kiss her. If it's the last chance I have, you'd better bet I'll grab it.

"Owen?" Her eyes are so full of confusion.

"How's your headache?"

"A lot better than it was. Painkillers and a day in bed helped. I'm looking forward to another big sleep tonight." Her lips twist. "Although, I'm sure you have other ideas."

"I always have other ideas when it comes to you." I grab her hands and lead her to the couch. "But first, there's something I need to talk to you about."

Her eyes well with tears, and her reaction bewilders me.

I reach up and stroke her cheek, catching a tear as it falls. "Why are you crying?"

"Is this it?" she asks.

Damn it. Damn my reputation. I'd give up the memory of every single girl I'd ever been with if it stopped this reaction in her. "Only if you're dumping me." I try to smile, but it comes out a bit wonky.

She still has this worried look in her eyes, as if she's not convinced. "Why would I?" Her voice shakes.

I take a deep breath. "I had some unexpected news today. I don't want it to cause us any issues because I love being with you, but I'm scared it will."

"What is it?"

"Can I show you? I don't know if I can find the words by themselves."

She nods.

I take her hand and stand. She follows suit, and I find myself looking into her eyes. I pull her to me and kiss her again. Her lips are as warm and welcoming as always and give me comfort when I need it.

"Owen," she whispers.

"There's something important I need you to see. *Someone.*"

Her eyebrows twitch, and the words get caught in my throat. *My daughter.*

I lead her up the hallway to the door of the spare room—Ava's room. Light from the hallway illuminates the bed, and there's Ava, her blonde hair spread across the pillow, her thumb in mouth.

"Ava?"

"She's my daughter."

Ginny's head spins back as if it's got a life of its own. "Your daughter?"

"I only found out today."

She raises her hand to cover her mouth. I pull the door to and walk down the hall, Ginny following me.

"Social services fucked around for a while." I hold my hands up in exasperation. "No, that's not exactly true. They didn't know, and when they found out, they brought her here."

"Oh my God."

I lick my lips. "So, if you want to walk away from me, I'll understand. It's not what I want, but this isn't what you signed up for."

She looks back toward the bedroom before refocusing on me. When she opens her mouth as if to talk and says nothing, it's the longest moment of my life. "To tell you the truth, I'm not sure what I signed up for anyway." She lets out a loud breath. "If this is you, I'll take it, Owen. I'll take all of it."

"Really?"

A smile spreads across her face. "It's you I want. This is your life."

Relief floods through me. "I thought you might change your mind."

She reaches for my face and runs her fingers through my stubble. "Taking responsibility for Ava says a lot about you. That you're opening your heart and your home to that little girl tells me that you're not as afraid of commitment as I thought you might be."

I capture her wrist in my hand and plant a kiss on it. "Ava's been through so much. And she deserves so much more than she's had the past few weeks."

"No matter the reason, you're a good man. One I'm proud to be with."

Pulling her into my arms, I lose myself in her kiss. How lucky am I to have found her?

"I know it's early, but can we go to bed?" she whispers.

As if I'd say no.

13

OWEN

The bed's cold when I wake, but it's still dark.

My alarm clock tells me it's a little after two. I could roll over and go back to sleep, but Ginny's absence worries me. Has she had second thoughts?

I stagger into the hallway, half asleep, and take a couple of steps before hearing a soft voice singing. Ginny's sitting on Ava's bed, stroking her hair and singing "The Owl and the Pussycat". It takes a moment, but she smiles when she notices me.

"She okay?"

Ginny nods. "She is now. I heard her crying and came in here to find she'd wet the bed. She was so scared she'd be in trouble."

"In trouble?"

"I get the feeling that somewhere along the way she's been with someone who's told her that. She kept saying

113

'Heidi said it was naughty.' Any idea who Heidi is?" She continues to stroke Ava's hair as she whispers.

I shrug. "At a guess, one of the places she stayed in the past few weeks."

"Well, I made sure she knows it's not naughty. She's four, and she's been through this crazy, traumatic experience. How could anyone tell her that?"

Walking to the bed, I squat beside it, and lay my hand on Ava's head. "I don't know, but she'll never be treated like that here."

"I found the spare sheets in the linen cupboard, and I had to dress her in what I could find. She's only got one pair of pyjamas. The washing machine's on."

"Thank you." Nodding, I sigh. "I'm sure there's some huge legal process to go through with the estate. For the moment, she's been left with only a small amount of stuff. I need to get her more things."

"We'll go shopping tomorrow."

My breath catches. "You don't have to do that."

"I can and I will. We'll go for a drive and get some new clothes." Ginny places her hand over mine. "We'll have her feeling like this is home in no time."

My heart surges with emotion, and I love this woman. I love what she does for me. I love what she's willing to do for us.

I take her by the hand. "Come here."

Leading her out to the hallway, I wrap my arms around her.

"Move in with us."

Her eyes widen. "What?"

"Not just for Ava. For me. I feel like tonight things changed for us, changed for the better."

"Me too. But I'm not going to move in. Not yet."

I swallow. "Okay."

"I need to know that you want me to move in for you, for us. Not just for Ava."

I flick a lock of her hair back. "What do you mean?"

"You now have a four-year-old, and all of a sudden the biggest commitment-phobe I know wants me to move in?"

Sighing, I stand and pull her into my chest. "It's a massive step for me, but if I'm going to do this with anyone, I want it to be you."

"Why me?"

I cup her chin, raising her gaze to meet mine. Even in the half light, those emerald eyes stir something in me. "Do you want to know why I've always steered clear of commitment?"

"You didn't answer my question."

"I promise I'll get to it."

She rolls her eyes. "Tell me."

"My dad had an affair."

Her mouth drops open. "Your father?"

"He doesn't know I know, but I saw him once. Wrong place, wrong time. I was twelve. My parents had their moments when they fought, but I thought they were solid. I realised I was wrong."

"I'm sorry," she whispers.

"I never wanted to do that to someone, never wanted to let them down. So I decided that I wouldn't settle down with one person. That way, no one gets hurt, right?"

"Oh, Owen." Her eyes brim with tears.

"And then I met you, and everything made sense. Maybe it's because I know for a fact I'd never stray. I love you."

Her breath hitches. "I love you too."

"You're the first woman I've ever said that to." I kiss her forehead as her brows twitch.

"Really?"

"Before you, I never wanted the morning after. I still don't know if saying 'I love you' is enough, because the way you make me feel? It's endless. It's like my heart is about a million times bigger, because that's what being with you does to me."

Her lower lip wobbles, and tears run down her cheeks.

"I'll wait however long it takes for you to be ready to move in with me. I'm not going anywhere."

Ginny wraps her arms around my neck and holds on tight. Maybe meeting her was destiny too, like all the pieces of my life coming together at once.

"You need to learn to be a father to Ava before we can take this further."

"I know," I whisper. "But I still want you to be part of my life."

She lets go and nods. "I'll still stay over some nights. It's just really important that you and Ava bond."

"Don't forget that Ava's going to have a couple of uncles I'm sure will be willing to babysit from time to time." I grin. "Not to mention cousins. Can you imagine Max's reaction to this?"

Ginny laughs. "She'll follow him everywhere."

"It'll give him a lesson on how much of a pest having a younger sister can be."

She nods.

"Let's go back to bed." I walk back into the bedroom, and press a kiss to Ava's forehead. She stirs, but her eyes stay closed. None of this feels real, but I guess we just have to take things as they come.

As I exit the room, I take Ginny's hand in mine, and lead her back to my room. She nestles in against my chest, and I close my eyes.

For the first time, my little flat feels like a family home.

GIGGLES FLOAT THROUGH THE AIR, and the sound of Ava and Ginny laughing makes me smile.

I climb out of bed and make my way to the living room doorway.

They've made up a bed on the couch, snuggling under a blanket while watching cartoons on television. Signs of breakfast sit on the coffee table. It all makes my heart full.

"Hey, you two."

"Morning, babe." Ginny raises her face for me to kiss, and I linger on her lips.

"How long have you been up?"

"Not that long. Ava was awake when I got up to use the bathroom, so I thought we'd get breakfast out of the way before we go shopping." She grimaces. "We do have the small problem of not having the right car seat for her."

"Shit."

"But there's a store in Carlstown that'll have them. We just have to get there."

I shake my head. "I'll call Adam and Lily and see if Rose has a suitable one we can steal."

Ginny nods. "I guess it depends on the type of seat they have, but that's a good idea."

"Can you imagine them when I ask for it?"

She laughs. "I'm guessing you haven't told them about Ava?"

"No one knows but you. And Mel."

"I bet she was surprised."

I nod. "You could say that. I'll give Lily a call now. The sooner we can get going, the better."

Picking up my phone, I call Lily.

"Hello?"

I grin at the sound of Max's voice. "Hey, Max. It's Owen. Is your mum there?"

"Mum, it's Owen," he yells. I hold my phone away from my ear and laugh.

"Owen?" Lily sounds concerned, but I guess it's because I don't call her often.

"Hey, Lily. I was wondering if I could ask you a favour?"

"Anything."

"I need to borrow a child's car seat for a few hours, and I was wondering about Rose's. Is it suitable for a four-year-old?"

Lily pauses. "Should be. We'll just need to adjust the harness, and you can use it forward facing. What's this all about?"

"There's something I need to tell you and Adam."

"Owen?"

"Can I come over and get the car seat? I'll explain then."

"Sure thing. I look forward to it."

I shove my phone in my pocket. "I'm just going to pop

over and pick up the car seat. Lily seems to think it'll be okay. We can drop it off on the way home."

"Sounds good. We'll keep entertained here for a while longer."

I smile, and make my way around the couch to Ava. "I'm just going out for a little while, and when I get back, we'll go for a car ride."

She nods.

"On the way home, you can come and meet Uncle Adam and Auntie Lily. They're going to love seeing you."

Her blue eyes widen. This is a kid who has no extended family. Or didn't until now. This has got to be scary and exciting.

"Be back soon, kiddo."

The thought of telling Adam and Lily about Ava makes me feel a mix of nervous and excited. Sure, I have concerns about my ability to parent, but that she's now got somewhere stable to live makes me determined to give her the best life possible.

Lily's standing beside the dining table when I enter the house with a quick knock on the open door, and her eyebrows shoot up at the sight of me.

"Why do you need a car seat?"

I let out a loud breath. "Hello to you too. Because I just found out I have a daughter. And she's living with me now."

"What?" Her mouth drops open.

"Cara and Ryan Mitchell's daughter. I'm her real father." I fist my hands. "Thankfully Cara left a will with that little piece of information. Ava's been bounced from home to home these past few weeks. Ginny's at home with her now while I sort out this seat."

"Oh, God, Owen." Lily sinks into a chair.

"I know. It's a lot to take in."

"You never suspected?"

I shrug. "Cara was happy. That's all I wanted. I didn't pay any attention to the timeline of it all. I'd well moved on by the time Ava was born."

"I'm glad it's you."

I frown. "What do you mean?"

"What would have happened if you weren't in the picture? What if Ava was Ryan's? She'd still be floating from family to family, but now she has her family."

Gulping, I nod. "You're right."

"If there's anything we can do, just let us know."

"Well, I need the car seat until we get one in Carlstown. But I will bring her back here to meet you."

Lily smiles. "I'd love that. I'll put Rose's seat in your car, but get the shop to show you how to fit the new one."

"I don't know if I'm up to this, Lily."

She stands, wrapping her arms around my waist. "You've always been more capable than you think. Don't sell yourself short."

"I know, but how the hell can I do this? It's huge."

Lily leans her head into my chest. "We'll be here if you need help, or even if you want to drop her off for some time out. How did Ginny take the news?"

"Surprisingly well. I thought she might freak out more, given that we've been trying to take things slow. But she took it in her stride, and the two of them are on the couch cuddled up under a blanket watching cartoons at the moment."

She chuckles. "That's good. I'm glad it hasn't disrupted you two. It's been good to see you both so happy."

Smiling, I kiss the top of her head. "We are happy."

"Bro." Adam appears in the doorway, cocking an eyebrow as he takes in the sight of me hugging his girl.

"Hey."

"Owen has some news," Lily says, letting go. "I'll transfer that seat to your car while you catch your brother up."

"Catch me up with what?"

My breath catches. Every time I tell this story, it gets a little more real, but it's still weird. "Long story short, I have a daughter."

His eyebrows twitch, but there's no shock on his face. "There's a surprise. I always wondered how many kids you might have out there."

I glare at him. "Don't be a dick."

"So, who?"

"Cara Mitchell."

His mouth falls open. "Shit."

"Yeah. Yesterday, my four-year-old daughter appeared on my doorstep. Poor kid's been bumped around these past few weeks, and I have no idea what to do, but I'm doing it."

A small smile appears on his face. "I guess she could do a lot worse than being a Campbell."

"Yeah, considering that neither Ryan or Cara seem to have any living relatives. I'm all she's got."

"Bollocks. She's got all of us."

I nod, and can't help but smile. "Yeah, she does. I'm just

stealing Rose's car seat for a bit while we go to Carlstown and buy one. She's got nothing, Adam."

His eyebrows knit together, annoyance all over his face. I know that look. He gets it when he thinks someone close to him has been screwed over. Since returning, Adam's been fiercely protective of the family he once walked away from. I think he'll spend the rest of his life trying to make up for leaving.

"Then we all have to make things better for her," he says.

"I agree."

His expression softens. "She'll be good for you."

I nod. "Maybe. It's all so weird and new right now. My immediate concern is that she knows that she's safe and won't be moved again."

He reaches over and grips my shoulder. "You know we're here if you need us."

"Lily said the same thing. You guys might regret saying that."

He laughs. "Never. I can't wait to meet your daughter."

<hr>

GINNY AND AVA play games on our journey. They play I Spy, and then count different-coloured cars as we get closer to town. It does my heart good to hear them both so happy.

It's been a little more than twenty-four hours since Ava arrived, and already she seems on the way to being settled.

"We'll go and get the clothes first. Then we'll get the car seat and they might help us fit it in the car," Ginny says.

"Yes, oh wise one."

She pinches my ear.

"Hey, cut that out."

"You're such a smart arse." She laughs.

"Such a smart arse," Ava parrots Ginny's words, and I laugh as Ginny slaps her hand across her mouth.

"I should know better. I'm sorry, Owen. Here I am teaching your daughter bad words."

I shake my head. "You'll keep. Ava, don't repeat Ginny's bad words."

Ava giggles. Something tells me she knows she's not supposed to say things like that. Her dad, her *other* dad, used to swear like a trooper. I would hazard a guess she's heard every bad word under the sun.

Pulling up outside the shopping centre, we get out of the car and head inside and toward the department store.

"I'll take her," Ginny says.

"Are you sure?"

She nods. "I'm sure I have better taste than you do."

I chuckle, planting a kiss on her cheek. "I bet you do. I'll go and take a look around, and meet you by the checkouts. Make sure she's got lots of everything."

"I'll sort it out, Owen. Don't worry."

For a moment, I watch Ginny and Ava disappear into the children's clothing section. I'm so glad I have Ginny with me, and not just because she can help with finding clothes. She's already brought so much stability to me, and with any luck, that will flow down to Ava.

I never thought I'd find myself here, but I have to admit, I'm in love. Ginny's exactly what we both need.

I walk toward the children's section, and pick up a night light. Ava didn't complain last night about the dark, but then again she didn't come looking for me when she wet the bed.

Maybe this will help comfort her. It doesn't take long for Ginny and Ava to return.

The basket in Ginny's arms is overflowing with clothing, and I shake my head as they approach. "Did you buy the whole store?"

Ava laughs. "No."

"It looks like it."

Ginny grins. "Come on, Ava. Let's go get all of this, and then Owen can buy us some lunch."

"You're not paying for that."

Her lips twitch. "Yeah, I am."

"She's *my* responsibility."

"I want to spoil her. God knows she deserves it."

I narrow my eyes. "I'll find a way to pay you back, and you won't even know it."

Ginny grins. "You can make it up to me tonight."

My body stirs at her comment, and my heart leaps. I need to adjust to Ava being with us, but it's like we're a little family. It's weird, and at the same time, it's wonderful.

I know I'm not alone in this, and although I have the support of Adam and Lily, it's Ginny who matters the most. It scared me I might lose her, but she's doing this with me.

"Ginny?" A tall, well-built man approaches. His eyebrows shoot up as he looks down at Ginny and Ava holding hands, and I don't miss his curious glance at me.

Is this the ex that treated her badly, or …?

Ginny beams. She shifts her gaze to me. "Owen, this is my brother, Kyle."

He holds out his hand. "Kyle Robinson."

I grasp it and shake. "Owen Campbell."

Ava shrinks behind Ginny's leg, but Kyle peeks around her. "And this is …?

"This is Ava. We're doing some clothes shopping," Ginny says.

"Wow. Looks like you bought the whole store."

Ava giggles.

"We were just getting these and then going for lunch. Want to join us?" I ask. I haven't met Ginny's family yet, but she's told me how protective her brothers are of her. It's a good opportunity to get on Kyle's good side.

"That'd be great. It seems there are a few things Ginny hasn't told me."

Ginny laughs. "I don't tell you everything."

"I know. Looks like there's plenty to catch me up on."

His tone isn't menacing, but it's clear he wants to know all about me and Ava.

"Then we'll do that over lunch." She raises her chin, almost looking down her nose at him. I suppress my smile, but my girl is in control of this exchange, no matter what her brother thinks.

"I'll meet you outside," he says.

She nods. "See you there."

When we get to the counter, I pull out my credit card, and Ginny shoots me a dirty look. "I told you, I'm paying."

"No, you're not."

"I am." She stands as tall as she can and pushes her chest out like she's trying to look tough. It makes me chuckle. "Owen, let me do this. You get her the car seat."

"Fine." I plant a kiss on her lips.

"Give me more of those later, and we'll call it even."

I look down as Ava slots her hand into mine. Her parents

had such an up-and-down relationship at times. Hopefully seeing Ginny and me happy is helping the settling-in process.

Her brother's waiting as we exit the store, and we all head toward the food court.

"I think I'm going to get a burger and fries. What do you guys want?" I ask.

"I want a salad." Ginny smiles.

"Crazy woman." Kyle laughs.

"It's my shout. What do you want?" I ask him.

"Thanks. Burger and fries would be good too."

I look at Ava. "Chicken nuggets and fries?"

She nods, and I ruffle her hair.

I pay, and we carry the trays of food to the table and get stuck in.

"So, how did you guys meet?" Kyle asks.

Ginny grabs my arm. "Owen and I met at his brother's wedding."

"There's something familiar about you," he says, narrowing his eyes.

I'm not sure if that's good or bad, given my chequered history with women.

His expression relaxes. "I thought I recognised you. The Copper Creek Bakery."

I grin. "That's me."

"In the summer, Jordan and I head out to the cove some weekends. It's such a great little beach there, and there are some hot girls."

I nod.

"We always stop at your bakery and buy meat pies. They're the best. Better than anything around here."

Ginny nudges my arm, looking at me with so much pride.

"Thanks."

We eat in silence for a while. Ginny steals half my chips, and I shake my head and smile at her. Something Kyle doesn't miss.

"So, you and my sister have been seeing each other."

I fix my gaze on him. "For the past couple of months."

"And you have a little girl."

I shoot a glance at Ava. She's got French fries hanging out of her mouth, and is completely engrossed in the toy Ginny bought her in the middle of all those clothes.

"Yeah, I do."

"What about her mum?"

Ginny's eyes widen, and she nods toward Ava. "Can we talk about this later?"

He nods. "Yeah. We should do a dinner at Mum and Dad's. They'd love to meet you, and honestly, Mum will go a bit crazy with your little girl."

"She really will." Ginny laughs.

"I'd love to." It's been years since I met a girl's parents. But then again, everything with Ginny's been different.

"Let's organise something. I know Jordan will be keen."

Ginny leans her head on my shoulder. "I did tell you I had *two* overprotective brothers. Didn't I?"

"You sure did." I plant a kiss in her hair.

"I guess this explains why you didn't move back home." Kyle takes another bite of his burger.

Ginny raises her head. "No," she says quietly.

"Is work any better?"

I don't know what to do. It's news to me that she was

even thinking about leaving Copper Creek. When I turn my head to look at her, she won't meet my eyes.

"It's still the same. But it's nothing, Kyle."

"It was enough to make you think about changing jobs."

I reach for her hand and squeeze it.

"Owen knows about it. Right?"

I clear my throat, a little annoyed that she never told me this. "Depends on what *it* is."

"Her creepy-as boss. She was so uncomfortable she thought about quitting and coming home." He fixes his gaze on Ginny. "You didn't tell Owen?"

Licking my lips, I focus on Ginny. Her expression is blank, but she squeezes my hand in return. "I know her boss. What's going on, Ginny?"

She shakes her head. "Nothing's going on. He just makes me really uncomfortable sometimes."

"How?"

Kyle frowns. "Do you not believe her?"

"I didn't say that. Given I didn't know anything about this, I want to know what's happening. I know both him and his wife, but if he's being inappropriate ..."

She sighs. "It's just the way he looks at me. And I'm not the only one. There's also innuendo. And then there's Michelle Marshall."

"Should I know that name?" I ask.

"She quit earlier in the year. There were rumours that he made a move on her, but she refused to talk about it, and nothing ever came of it."

"It worries me that you didn't tell Owen about it," Kyle says.

"It bothers me," I say. The last thing I want is for Ginny's brother to think we're keeping things from each other, but I can't help my reaction to this.

Ginny wraps her arms around my waist and snuggles in. "I'm not sure if it's just me being paranoid, or if it's an actual thing. Being with you makes me feel safer."

"You moving in with me would make me feel safer."

Kyle's eyes widen. "Woah. You're *that* serious?"

"Yes." I smile at Ginny.

"But, we're not ready for it just yet." She looks at me with so much love, it takes my breath away.

I look over at Ava. She's eaten all her food, and now she's hugging her toy to death. "That teddy's pretty cool, isn't it?"

Her eyes widen, and she nods.

"Now you've got your old one and your new one." Ginny reaches over and strokes Ava's hair.

Ava hops off her seat and walks around the table to me. She shoves the teddy in my face. "I love him."

"I'm sure you do." I slip an arm around Ginny's shoulders. "It was nice to meet you, Kyle. We should get going and take this car seat back in case Lily needs it."

"Good to meet you, too. I'll talk to Mum about organising a get-together, and no doubt she'll be in touch with Ginny." He holds out his hand, and I shake it.

I nod. "I'll look forward to it."

And I do. The thought of meeting Ginny's family makes me warm inside. I think Kyle, Jordan and I will get along fine. We all want to protect Ginny.

I want to be a part of that family.

14

OWEN

I STASH ROSE'S CAR SEAT IN THE BOOT OF THE CAR, ALONG with the bags of shopping. Ava's ended up with an extensive wardrobe thanks to Ginny, and I've barely paid for a thing. It's irritating, and I'll find a way to pay Ginny back, but it makes my heart sing to see both Ginny and Ava so happy.

The salesperson from the baby shop shows me how to fit Ava's new seat, and once it's in, Ava sits in it, presiding over the car like a queen.

"This is my seat?" she asks.

I laugh. "It's all yours. We can take Rose's seat back and maybe you can meet her."

"Who's Rose?"

I smile. "She's your cousin. My brother's little girl."

"Can I play with her?"

"Sure. She's only one though, so she's smaller than you."

Her eyes widen, and my heart warms to see her excited

and happy. It's a far cry from the little girl sitting in the chair and swinging her feet only yesterday.

"And you can meet Max. He's quite a lot older than you, but I bet he'll be really happy to meet you. He's got a pet dog, Lucky."

She claps, and I stand as I finish buckling her in.

"You're not bad at this," Ginny says.

"I don't think I'm good at it yet either." I laugh.

"You've accomplished more in the past day than a lot of people probably would have. Ava's happy. That's what matters."

"I love that you two have bonded too. The whole thing's such a shock, but everything seems to be slotting into place." I peck her on the cheek, opening her door for her.

She smiles as she climbs in, and I close the door behind her.

Time to go home.

AVA FALLS asleep on the way back, only to wake as we pull into Adam and Lily's driveway.

"Just in time." I laugh. "We're at Uncle Adam's place."

Her eyes widen, and I'm not sure if it's in excitement or fear.

I open the boot of the car while Ginny lets Ava out of her car seat. Ava hugs her teddy-bear tight as we walk toward the house.

"That didn't take long." Adam opens the door, and steps back to let us all in. "Lily's in the living room. Just put the seat by the door, and I'll take it out a bit later."

Lily sits on the couch, and smiles as she sees us. Adam follows us in.

"Ava, this is Uncle Adam and Auntie Lily."

Lily smiles. "Hi, Ava. It's very nice to meet you."

Ava wraps her arms around my waist, hiding behind me and peeking out at Lily.

"Ava." Adam squats in front of me. "Would you like to meet Max and Rose? They're your cousins."

She takes a step forward, looking up. I nod. Ava holds her arms up for me to pick her up, and I scoop her into my arms.

Adam stands. "Fair enough. Rose is having a nap, but she should be awake soon. I'll go and get Max."

He disappears up the hallway, returning with my nephew in tow.

"Max, this is your cousin, Ava," Adam says.

Max stares at her. "Cousin?"

"This is my daughter," I say.

He grins. "Hi, Ava." His gaze shifts to me. "You never said you had a daughter."

"I just found out myself."

"Like my dad did with me."

Lily places her hands on his shoulders. "Just like that. Why don't you introduce Ava to Lucky? I bet she'll love him."

"Come on, Ava," Max says. Ava scrambles to be let down again. Max holds out his hand, and Ava takes it without question, only turning when they get to the back door. I nod.

"He'll take good care of her. Want a coffee, you two?" Adam asks.

"I'd love one," Ginny says.

"Take a seat, and I'll bring some in."

He winks at Lily before heading toward the kitchen. I

flop down on the couch beside her, Ginny sitting on my other side.

"She's gorgeous. I love how she had no problems with Max," Lily says.

"Kids always seem more comfortable with other kids." Ginny leans forward. "She's quite shy, but I think she's met a lot of people these past few weeks, so maybe it's made it easier to come out of her shell a bit quicker."

Lily fixes her gaze on me. "It's still weird to think of you being a dad. I wonder why Cara didn't tell you."

I shrug. "If I'd known the truth, I would have been happy for her."

"Maybe she thought you would have wanted to be involved."

I nod. "Maybe. It makes me sad she didn't confide in me, but she could have."

Ginny leans her head on my shoulder, linking my fingers in hers. "At least now you can do right by her."

"I can. It's not going to be easy, but I'll do the best job I can looking after Ava," I say.

"Well, you've got our support too. Don't ever forget that," Lily says.

A shriek comes from outside, and I'm on my feet in an instant.

I race to the door, and laugh when I see what the problem is. Ava's met Lucky.

From what I can see, he's knocked her over in the excitement of the kids playing, given the way he's panting over her and nudging her arm.

"What happened?" I ask.

"We were playing with the ball and Lucky accidentally ran into Ava," Max says.

She's not scared, she's shrieking with laughter, and I shake my head, walking down the steps and holding out my hand for her to take.

"Looks to me like you're doing just fine," Lily calls from the door.

Ava grins as she takes my hand and pulls herself up.

Maybe this will all work out.

<hr>

AT HOME, Ava eats her spaghetti and meatballs with enthusiasm, smears of pasta sauce and cheese everywhere.

I shake my head. "I think you might need to have a bath to get all that off."

She laughs.

"You sort that out. I'll clear the dishes," Ginny says.

"Are you sure you don't want to do it?"

She shakes her head. "I can't be here for every bath time, and you need to get used to doing these things for her."

"Fair enough. Come on, Ava. Let's get some of those new pyjamas." Her new clothes were all washed and dried when we came home, ready and waiting for her to start using them.

Ava licks her hands, and I roll my eyes, chuckling at the sight. My flat is usually spotless, though that's aided by me either working or not being here. I'm going to have to get used to a little mess.

She picks out her new pink pyjamas and Disney Princess underwear, and we head into the bathroom. The bath doesn't get used a lot, but I guess that's another change.

"Do you want a shower instead?"

She shakes her head. "I don't like the shower."

Great. I thought I could get through this quickly.

I run some water in the bath while she puts the lid down on the toilet and sits on it, swinging her feet. How many other aspects of normal life have I not thought of? It's not like this is going to be her one and only bath.

"Is everything okay in here?" Ginny appears in the doorway.

"Just waiting for the water to be deep enough."

"You're doing a great job, Dad." She pokes her tongue out at me. "You okay, Ava?"

Ava nods.

"I'm just going to go and load the dishwasher. Call me if you need me."

She disappears before I can say another word. Ginny's doing the right thing in pushing me to do this. I can't depend on her for everything. It's up to me to get all these everyday things under control.

I run my fingers through the water. On the rare occasion I have a bath, I like it steaming hot, but I have to think about Ava's safety. It seems warm enough, but not too warm.

"Ava, put your hand in here and tell me if it's okay."

"Can I have bubbles?"

I shake my head. "Not tonight, but next time I go to the supermarket, we can get some bubble bath."

Her lower lip wobbles.

"I usually have a shower, sweetheart. But I promise we'll have bubbles next time. Is it warm enough? Not too hot?"

She grins. "It's good."

"Then let's get your clothes off and hop in."

When she struggles with her T-shirt, I help pull it over her head, and hold her hand as she steps into the bath.

She looks down at the water and pouts.

"I'm sorry, Ava. There are some things you'll have to teach me about, like the bubbles."

She sits, and I grab a flannel from the cupboard and give it to her before collecting the body wash from the shower. At the scent, she wrinkles up her nose.

"Okay. Little girl body wash, too. I'm not used to females being in my house."

Ava laughs. "Ginny's here."

"Ginny only stays sometimes. Maybe she'll stay more with you here."

"I like Ginny." Ava hands me the flannel, and I take a breath. She's still covered in sauce and has barely cleaned anywhere.

"Me too. Come here." I gently rub the red, drying sauce from around her mouth, and tap the tip of her nose for the blob that made it there.

She giggles as I wash her jawline, collecting the last of the mess. "Does that tickle?"

She nods.

I rinse out the flannel in the bath water, and add some more body wash before rubbing her back and then her legs. "Wanna get your tummy?"

Ava grabs the wash cloth from me and rubs it all over her chest. "All clean."

"Are you? Shouldn't we wash your hair?"

"Will it smell yucky?"

I laugh. "Tell you what—how about we add shampoo for you to the shopping list."

She nods.

After a bit of splash time, I help her out of the bath and wrap a towel around her. She giggles as I dry her off.

"Are you ticklish?"

Ava nods.

I tap her on the nose. "I'm sorry."

She shivers.

"Let's get you dry and dressed. You'll be warm, then."

I hold her clothing as she steps into it. Buttoning up her pyjama top, I grin. "Did I do a good job?"

She nods.

"Let's go and see what Ginny's doing."

Ava sprints from the room, leaving me standing there. It's clear she adores Ginny. The two of them have become close in an insanely short amount of time.

When I reach the living room, Ginny's standing in the middle of it. Ava's arms are around her neck, and she's got her legs hooked around Ginny's waist.

"That looks comfortable."

Ginny laughs. "I heard her call my name, and she launched herself at me. How could I say no?" She kisses Ava's temple. "Are you ready for bed?"

"Can I have a story?" Ava asks.

"I'm pretty sure I can think of one."

My heart swells watching them. To think I was worried that Ginny would change her mind about us when she found out about Ava. Of course she didn't. We're in too deep for her to do that.

"Say goodnight to Owen, and I'll put you to bed." Ginny walks toward me, and I can see the discomfort in her face.

"Want me to carry her?" I ask.

"It's okay. It's not far."

I run my fingers through Ava's hair and kiss her cheek. "Night, sweetheart. See you in the morning."

She rests her head on Ginny's shoulder, and the two of them make their way up the hall.

They both have my heart.

IT DOESN'T TAKE LONG for Ginny to make her way back, and she's got a smile on her face a mile wide.

"I think she was exhausted after the drive, and the food. She fell asleep about thirty seconds into her story. I'll have to get her some books."

"What was the story about?"

Ginny sits beside me on the couch, looping her arms around my waist. "It was about a princess in a castle, and the handsome prince coming to rescue her."

"Is there some hidden meaning behind that?"

She laughs. "Whether you know it or not, you're saving her, Owen. Saving her from a life of being unsettled and not knowing what's coming next. I don't know if she gets it either. We need to make sure she knows the rug isn't going to be pulled out from under her feet."

"She's doing really well." I look into Ginny's eyes. "And she loves you."

"I think 'love' is a bit too far. But she's probably felt safer and more wanted in the last twenty-four hours than she has the last few months. She knows she can trust you, and I'm the lady who gave her cookies at the funeral."

I laugh. "You're probably right. Are you sure you don't want to move in with us?"

Ginny lets out a loud breath, and sucks her bottom lip in. "You need to become her new normal. She'll become more attached to me if I'm around all of the time, and there's nothing wrong with that, but it has to be you. You have to be the centre of her universe."

I link my fingers in hers. "You're more than just an attachment."

"Maybe. But we don't know what will happen to us long-term. I don't want her getting in too deep with me in case things don't work out, and she has to deal with another loss."

My chest tightens at the idea of losing Ginny. She means more to me than she'll ever know. Not only has she brought me love, but she's settled me in ways I never thought possible. I miss her when we're not together, and my heart leaps when she walks into a room.

Ginny's given me a life.

I can't lose her.

"That won't happen."

She looks at me with those eyes that bore into my soul. "You don't know that."

"Yeah, I do. I know you think I just want you to live with us because Ava's in my life now, but it's not the only reason. It's because I want to be with you, and only you."

Her eyelashes flutter, and it sends my heart racing. "I know you say that now ..."

"No. This is it."

"Owen, we've known each other two months."

"I've known it all along. You were who I was meant to meet." I run my free hand through my hair. "I've been thinking about this a lot."

Ginny smiles.

"I'm serious, Gin. The wedding, meeting you, the accident. Fuck, my heart was broken seeing that car, and knowing Ava had no one. But you were there when I needed you, and you stuck around. Now, what I have with you is unlike anything I've ever had before and that was before I knew Ava was mine."

Tears form in her eyes.

"You have no reason to believe this, but I don't even have to try with you. And I don't mean that I'm not going to do what I can to show you how I feel, but being with you is so easy."

She squeezes my fingers with hers. "Is it me? Or was it that everything else seemed too hard?"

That wasn't a question I'd anticipated, and I stare at her, unable to formulate an answer.

"You might have met me that same night, but when you came back to the wedding, you'd lost someone you cared deeply about. And I was there."

I shake my head. "That's not it."

"Maybe not, but how do I know? What if it had been someone else. Would you feel this way about them?"

Letting out a loud sigh, I shake my head again. "No. I saw you before I left the wedding. You were so sweet and charming, and your laugh made me smile. It was easy with you from the start. That's how I know."

Tears roll down her cheeks, and I reach out to catch them

with my finger. "No one else. It's you. You're so deep in here, I couldn't get rid of you if I wanted to." I pat my heart.

Despite her tears, she chuckles.

"That's better. Don't ever be sad with me. I'm not expecting you to jump in and be a mother to Ava—that's not why I'm with you. But I do appreciate everything you're doing for her. I'll need all the help I can get."

Her lips twitch. "I'll do whatever you two need me to."

"We both just need you." I wrap my arms around her as she leans into me, and brush my lips against her temple.

"You have me," she whispers.

"Let's go to bed. I'll show you how much I need you." As I stand, our earlier conversation springs to mind. "After you tell me what's going on with Nathan Webster?" Reaching for her hand, I help her to her feet.

"Nothing's going on. He's just a bit too friendly at times."

"Define 'too friendly'."

She shrugs. "He gets personal. Just enough to make you unsure of whether he's being creepy or looking out for you." Licking her lips, she sighs. "He spoke to me about you."

"He did what?"

"I can't run away from your reputation, Owen, even if I know you're different with me." She places her hand on my chest. "I'm not going to listen to anything other than my heart, and it tells me that what we have is something special. I wouldn't still be here if it wasn't."

I pull her into my arms and close my eyes. It pisses me off that other people have stuck their noses into our business, but at least it's because they care what happens to Ginny.

But I'll hurt Nathan Webster if he goes near my girl again.

15

OWEN

In the morning, we all have breakfast together before Ginny goes home to get some marking done and have some time to herself.

While she's not moving in, she'll spend tonight with us to help settle Ava in, and we'll have breakfast together again. I'm loathe to tackle the subject of her living with us again as she's made her views clear. And she's right. I do need to work out how to take care of Ava by myself.

Even if I think Ginny's the one.

The last thing I expect is Drew and Hayley on my doorstep in the middle of the afternoon.

"What are you two doing here?" I haven't seen them since their wedding day, it's so good to have them here.

He grins. "I've got something exciting to tell you. Wanted to do it in person."

I usher him in, and he walks into the living room,

followed by Hayley. As she draws level, I grab her arm and plant a kiss on her cheek. "I've got news for you too."

Drew spins back to face me before sitting on the couch. "If it's that you're with Ginny Robinson, I already know that news."

Hayley laughs as she sits beside him. "Lily's really excited about that one."

I shake my head. "No. It's not that." Sitting opposite, I lean forward.

"So, what's going on with you two?" They wear the same silly grins they did on their wedding day. Either that hasn't worn off or they're up to something else.

Drew grins. "We're having a baby."

My mouth drops. "No way. That's awesome."

Drew's always been one who wanted kids. He became an obstetrician because of the complications with Max's birth, and always harboured a wish to have his own. That it's with Hayley makes me happy. She really is the other half of him.

"Two babies." Hayley raises her palm to cover her mouth as she giggles.

"Twins?"

Drew nods. "Turns out I have uber-potent sperm."

"Dude, I do not want to know about your sperm."

He laughs.

"I need to show you my news. Hang on a second."

Drew's eyebrows raise as he looks at me, and I walk up the hallway to Ava's room. She's playing on the floor with the toys Ginny bought her.

"Hey, Ava. Want to come and meet Uncle Drew and Auntie Hayley?"

Her eyes widen, and she nods slowly.

"Come on."

I hold out a hand and she takes it, her teddy bear clutched tight in her other hand. We've come a long way, even since yesterday. With Ginny's help, Ava's trust in me has grown.

Drew stares at me as I enter the room, Ava in tow. Hayley beams.

"Drew, Hayley, this is Ava." I sit back on the chair and Ava sits on my lap. "She's my daughter."

Neither of them look surprised, and I swallow.

"How … why is she with you?" Drew finally asks.

"It's a long story, but I wanted you to meet her."

Hayley leans over. "Hi, Ava. I'm Hayley. It's very nice to meet you."

Ava leans against me, burying her face in my chest.

"What do you have there?" Hayley asks.

Ava sits back up. "Ginny bought me a new teddy-bear. I've still got my old one, but it's falling apart. And she bought me so many clothes, and …"

I chuckle. Clearly, she feels comfortable enough to start talking. I'm just not sure if she'll ever stop.

"Did you two want to stay for dinner?" I ask Drew.

He nods. "That would be great. We were going to visit Mum and Dad after this to tell them our news, but I called Dad to let him know we were coming, he mentioned Mum's not having a good day. I'd prefer not to put more pressure on him."

"Ginny should be back soon. She's trying not to smother us."

"I guess you have to get some time together." Drew shoots a glance at Ava.

"Yeah. I asked Ginny to move in, but she thinks I'm trying to make her some sort of surrogate mother."

He smirks. "Well, it's not like you've ever got as far as moving in with someone before."

Ava's already shifted to Hayley's lap, and is completely involved in telling her the story of what's happened since yesterday.

I lower my voice. "She's not like anyone else. All this has complicated things, but we're still seeing each other."

"So, you didn't say why she's staying with you. It must be weird for her."

I take a deep breath, and lean closer to Drew. "Remember that accident I had to leave your wedding reception for?"

He nods.

"Car versus truck. Ava was the only survivor."

"That was over two months ago, and you didn't say anything?"

I grit my teeth. As much as having her has turned things upside down, the thought of her moving from place to place still drives me nuts. "It took the authorities a while to sort their shit out, and I had no clue she was mine. Ava was put into care, and lived with several different people."

His mouth drops open. "No. That's awful."

"She's picked up some weird shit along the way. The first night, Ginny got up and heard her crying. Ava had wet the bed and was too scared to tell us. Someone had told her it was naughty."

Drew leans back. "Jesus. I would have thought that given she lost both her parents, that sort of thing would be par for the course."

"It must be. Anyway, I'm just going to have to adjust.

Having some warning would have been great. I didn't even know I had a kid."

There it is—a flash of guilt in his eyes.

"Did you know?" *How could he?*

His eyes dart from side to side. "That's a long story in itself."

"Tell me."

He clears his throat. "Hayley helped Cara deliver Ava."

My gaze shoots to my sister-in-law. I should be angry, but she's got Ava wrapped around her little finger already, and building relationships has to be important for Ava. It'd be helpful if kids came with an instruction manual, but I just have to work this stuff out.

"And you guys didn't think you should tell me?"

Drew lets out a sigh. "I wanted to. But Hayley would get in trouble for breaking patient confidentiality. I felt like I was stuck in the middle."

"A heads up would have been nice. If Cara and Ryan were happy, I wouldn't have done anything. It just would have been good to know. Damn it, Drew. If I'd known I would have fought from day one, and maybe she wouldn't have been shipped around for *two months*."

He nods, guilt written all over his face. "I know, but I couldn't. Shit. If I'd known that night who was in that accident ..."

I nod. "I guess I understand. It still pisses me off."

"Yeah, I bet it does. At least she's with you now. I bet she's real happy to have moved to Candyland."

Laughing I shake my head. "She's not going to live on cookies."

"Does she know that?"

Ava's still talking, describing our trip to buy clothing, and offering to show Hayley her room. The expression on Hayley's face is one of complete enchantment. She looks up and meets my gaze. *"She's gorgeous."* She mouths the words before shifting her attention back to Ava.

The door opens, and I grin at the sight of Ginny.

As if everything else is forgotten, Ava leaps from the couch and runs to her, throwing her arms around Ginny's waist as Ginny drops her bag beside the door.

"Oh, what a tackle." Ginny laughs. If she's trying to avoid Ava getting attached to her, it's way too late for that.

Ava raises her face and smiles, and Ginny bends to kiss her forehead. "What are you doing?"

"Talking. A lot." I laugh.

"Good." She smiles at Drew and Hayley. "Hi, guys."

"How are you, Ginny?" Drew asks.

"Good. Things are a bit crazy, but good."

Ava runs back to the couch, picking up the conversation where she left off with Hayley, and I shake my head in amusement. I get up and walk toward the door.

"Hey," Ginny says. She wraps her arms around my waist, and I give her a tender kiss.

"I missed you," I whisper.

"I wasn't gone that long."

"The more you stay, the more I hate it when you leave."

She cups my face. "Coming from you, that's a big call."

"It's true."

"Well, I'm staying tonight, and it should be a quiet one. With how excited Ava is, I bet she crashes early. It'll be nice to have some time together."

"It will be."

"How's she been with Drew and Hayley?"

I let out a sigh. "She took to Hayley in seconds."

Ginny laughs. "It figures. Hayley is such a lovely person."

"They knew."

She shoots me a confused look. "Knew?"

"Drew and Hayley knew about Ava. They knew, and they didn't tell me."

"How?"

"Hayley was there at Ava's birth. Cara told her."

Ginny rubs my back. "I guess she had to keep it confidential."

"I get that. It just grates a little that Drew knew and didn't say anything."

She licks her lips. "What would you have done if he had?"

I shrug. "Maybe nothing while they were alive. It just would have been nice to know. Maybe then Ava wouldn't have had to float from place to place until she came here."

Ginny smiles. "At least she's here now. And she has everything she could ever need. Give her time and those few weeks until she ended up here will be long forgotten."

"How'd I find someone so smart?" I press my lips to hers again.

"I guess you're just lucky." Ginny grins, and I laugh, giving her a squeeze before letting her go. She walks toward Hayley.

"Ginny, it's so good to see you." Hayley smiles. I love how easily Hayley's slipped into our family. It's as if she's always been here.

"You too. How was your honeymoon?" Ginny sits on a recliner beside the couch.

"Amazing. So relaxing. I didn't really want to come home."

I plant myself back on the other recliner, and smile as the ladies settle into chatting. Ava takes a run at me, launching herself onto my lap.

"What are you doing?" I laugh.

She giggles. "Sitting with you."

"She's gorgeous, Owen," Drew says. "Clearly, she takes after her mother."

I flick a lock of Ava's hair behind her ear. "I don't know. The more I look at her, the more I can see Max and Rose in there. She's definitely a Campbell."

"You seem very happy to be here." Drew smiles at Ava.

Ava loops her arms around my neck. This whole thing weirds me out, but that she's that comfortable with me already is going to help a lot down the track. Maybe it's just the relief of being with someone she now knows, someone who was there for her when she needed it. Whatever it is, she hugs me tight, and it warms my heart.

"I was there the night …" The sentence doesn't need to be finished. Drew knows what I mean.

"Of course."

"We hung out together, so little Miss Ava knew me. I think that's helped."

Ava rests her head against my shoulder. While she chatted up a storm with Hayley, she seems a bit more reserved around Drew.

"Did you know this is your Uncle Drew?" I ask her.

She looks up at me and nods.

"You've got four uncles and two aunts now. Plus, a couple of cousins."

Ava smiles.

"You've got a big family, Ava," Drew says.

She clings tighter to my neck.

"Ava met Adam and Lily yesterday. Today's probably a bit overwhelming." I stroke her hair. "I'm so glad Ginny's here. They've taken a real shine to each other, and it's helping ease the transition."

Ava holds up her teddy-bear. "Ginny bought this for me yesterday," she says to Drew.

"Did she? It's a very nice teddy. Did you know you're getting more cousins? Auntie Hayley's having two babies."

Ava's eyes widen. "Two babies?"

Drew nods. "You and Owen will have to come and visit us when they're born. We've got plenty of room, and a pool."

"And Ginny."

He laughs. "Yes, and Ginny. You're all welcome."

She climbs down off my lap, and within seconds is on the couch chatting with Drew.

Looking around the room, I smile.

I never thought I could be so content.

16

OWEN

The first week's tough.

I juggle everything. Getting up at four as usual, taking a break at seven to give Ava breakfast. She spends the day between the television in the living room when I take a break and the bakery. I need to sort something a bit more structured out for her, but it's all a bit overwhelming.

Thursday's usually our busiest day. It's the day the supplies arrive, and when I do an inventory to see what we need for the next week. Lily picks up Ava and takes her for the afternoon. Out of habit, I keep checking the living room to see what she's doing anyway.

The countdown to the weekend begins. Ginny will be with us. She pops in during the week, but doesn't stay, and I don't ask her to. She knows she has an open invitation.

On Saturday, the plan is to take both Ava and Ginny to meet my mother and father.

Hayley's initial meeting with my parents went really

badly. So badly, her reaction to it led to her and Drew breaking up, albeit temporarily.

I'm wary of taking Ginny there, but introducing Ava to them might help distract my mother. I need to hold onto that hope and be prepared to bail if it doesn't work.

My heart's beating fast as I pull into the driveway. I squeeze Ginny's hand as I lead her and Ava into the house.

"I'm here," I call out.

The house is quiet.

"Did you not let them know first?" Ginny whispers.

"I called Dad. They know we're coming."

I keep hold of Ginny's hand as I lead her to the door. Ava's on my other side, hanging back a little.

When we reach the living room door, Ginny goes through first, Ava trailing behind.

I'm right behind, smiling at the sight of my parents. Mum sits in her favourite chair, Dad on the couch. "Mum, Dad. This is Ginny. And I'd like you to meet Ava."

Dad's expression warms as I give Ava's hand a little tug and she peeks around the corner. "Hi, Ginny and Ava."

Mum, who's had permanent resting bitch face from even before she got sick, gives me the biggest surprise with her expression. Her lips wobble as she lays eyes on my daughter for the first time, and her mouth falls open. "She's yours?"

I nod. "I only just found out, and she's come to live with me."

"Oh, Owen."

I hold my breath, waiting for something snarky to come out of her mouth.

"She's beautiful."

Ava squeezes my hand.

"Come on. Do you want to meet your grandma and grandad?"

Her eyes widen, and she nods.

I take a step into the living room, and in an instant, Ava's arms are wrapped around my leg. We slowly make our way to the couch, and I sit, pulling her up beside me.

"Hello, Ava." Dad gives her a smile, and she leans against me, planting her thumb in her mouth. Ginny sits beside me.

"We're still getting used to each other, but she's doing really well."

Mum fixes her gaze on me. "Who's her mother?"

Dad stands, walking over to the couch. "Hey, Ava. Want to come for a walk? We have a big garden out the back and lots of pretty flowers. What's your favourite colour?"

"Purple," she whispers, removing her thumb from her mouth.

"I think there are some purple flowers out there. Want to look?"

Ginny smiles. "I might have to go for a walk too." She squeezes my bicep.

Ava looks at me with wide eyes, and I nod. "It's okay. Go with Grandad and Ginny."

I swear my dad's chest puffs up when I call him that, and it makes me smile. There's a bond there, ready to be formed, if Ava gives him the chance.

Ava lets go of my arm, and Dad holds out his hand for her to take. She takes another look at me, and I nod again. "I'll be right here when you want to come back."

There's hesitancy on her face, but she slowly reaches for Dad's hand, and pushes herself off the couch. One last look back at me at the door, and she disappears into the kitchen, Ginny right behind her.

I turn back to Mum. "Her mother was Cara Mitchell."

My mother's mouth falling open tells me I don't need to explain what happened to Ava's mother. "Oh, that poor girl."

"I had no idea, Mum." Shaking my head, I then bury it in my hands. "I was there the night Cara died, and I took care of Ava. Then I handed her off to go into care for two months before the social worker turned up and told me. She's been through so much."

"Well, at least you're here for her now."

I nod, looking back at her. "I'm not sure what I'm doing."

Mum chuckles. "No one is. We all get things right, and we all get things wrong. You're no exception." She leans forward. "You'll work it out. She's a lovely little girl."

"You know, you have two other grandchildren. They're just as precious as Ava."

She nods. "I know. And I have a lot of regret where they're concerned. I'm not sure if Adam will ever forgive me for what I did."

I sigh. "I'll talk to Adam. Maybe we can sort something out."

She leans back, and there's pain in her eyes. "Don't hold your breath. You're a good boy for suggesting it, but I don't think things will be better between us anytime soon. I can't make things right. It's too late."

I shrug. "I don't believe that for a second. Your grandchildren deserve to get to know you before ..."

Mum gives me a faint smile. "I know you're trying to be helpful, but nothing will be resolved between Adam and me before I die." She lets out a loud breath. "It's lovely to see you, and your daughter is beautiful, but I think I need to take a nap."

Nodding, I stand as she does. "Do you need any help?"

"I'll be fine."

I press a kiss to her cheek. "Take care, Mum. I'll work on Adam."

She raises her hand to cup my cheek. "I'm proud of you, Owen. I'm proud of all you boys. Even if it doesn't show sometimes."

"I know. I'll bring Ginny back sometime, too. You guys were so distracted by Ava that you didn't really get to talk to her."

"That would be nice."

I watch as she makes her way up the hallway toward the bedroom. It's clear she's going downhill, and I don't know how much longer she'll have. As much as she drives all of us crazy, we love her.

Stepping outside, I smile at the sight of my dad with Ava and Ginny walking toward the house.

Dad is more animated than I've seen him in a long time. Ava's got a firm hold on his hand, and she's swinging his arm as they walk. Ginny grins as I approach.

"Your dad's been telling us all about you." She laughs.

I roll my eyes. "Don't believe a word he says."

"I got a purple flower." Ava holds out her hand, a large bloom between her fingers.

"That's very pretty. Did Grandad show you the whole garden?"

She nods.

"Lucky. We'll have to put it in a glass when we get home. I don't think I have any vases. But a glass is enough to hold one flower." I turn to Dad. "We're going to get going. Mum's gone for a nap."

He nods. "It's happening more often these days."

"I'll bring Ava and Ginny back soon. Give me a call when Mum's up to visitors."

Dad grabs hold of my arm. "Any time you need me to look after Ava, I'm here."

"Thought you might be. I spoke to Mum about getting you two together with Adam and Lily. It needs to happen, Dad."

He nods. "I've seen them from time to time. At the wedding, and when Hayley left town. They're polite to me, but I want more. Your mother does too, although I doubt she'll admit it."

"She just says it's too late."

"Maybe it is."

I take Ava's hand. "We need to try. If anything, this whole thing has shown me more than ever how important family is."

Ginny looks at me with so much pride, and I raise an eyebrow. Maybe it's because every day I spend with Ava and Ginny, I become a better man.

Or at least I'm trying to become better.

OUR DRIVE HOME IS QUIET, and it's not until I pull into my driveway that I realise Ava's asleep in the back seat.

I smile as I unbuckle the harness.

"Want me to unlock?" Ginny asks, holding her hand out for the keys.

"That's a great idea. An even better idea is me giving you a key to my place."

She grins. "That's a big commitment right there."

Laughing softly, I hand her the keys and lift Ava out of her seat. She wriggles before looping one arm around my neck and snuggling into my chest.

I follow Ginny into the house, and take Ava through to her room. Today was good for her. I'm still not quite settled into the fact that this is my life now, but things are pretty close to perfect.

Placing her on the bed, I plant a kiss on her forehead before leaving the room.

Ginny's sitting on the couch when I get to the living room, and I join her. "That was a quick visit."

"Mum was a bit off-colour. We had a short talk, but I've taken you both to meet them, so at least that's done."

"So, your mum doesn't get on with Adam and Lily?" she asks.

We've not had this conversation as it's just not come up. "There's a lot of history there, and Mum's on the wrong side of it."

She sighs. "That sucks. Your mum was at Drew and Hayley's wedding, wasn't she?"

I nod. "She was, but Adam and Lily steered well clear of her. It's not an easy situation, and I guess taking Ava to meet her brought it home."

"Your mum and dad really loved her."

I grin. "They did. Dad misses out, too. He and Adam have a bit of a relationship, but it doesn't translate into him spending time with his grandchildren. At least he can spend time with Ava."

Ginny twists her mouth, and I raise my eyebrows.

"What's going on in that head of yours?"

"Your parents were really nice. I thought your mother would be a lot scarier."

I chuckle. "I think Ava being there spared you the third degree. Drew and Hayley broke up after their first visit together."

Her eyes widen. "You're kidding."

"Nah. Mum gave them a hard time about a long-distance relationship apparently, and how this town was too small for her big doctor son or something. Hayley was already stressed about the distance, and it all blew up." I lean over. "Introducing you did worry me. If anything, I think you're more sensitive than Hayley is. But you dodged a bullet."

She grins. "I'm thankful for that."

"Me too." *I've never been so relieved.* "Mum was never quite this bad. Not that I remember. She's facing her own mortality, and I'm not sure she likes what she sees."

Ginny lets out a loud breath. "That's got to be hard."

"It is. But I think they're just taking it as it comes. There are some days when I visit and she's in bed and too tired to get up. Today was a good day, and I think our little trip was good for her." I take Ginny's hand and squeeze it. "She got to meet my family, however brief our visit."

The look of love in her eyes is unmistakable.

"Thank you for taking me. It makes me feel closer to you."

I lick my lips. "Ava's asleep. So how about getting a lot closer to me?" Leaning back on the arm of the couch, I pull Ginny until she's on top of me. "What about this?"

"Well, I am really close." Her green eyes sparkle, and I lose myself in them as I take her in.

"Will you stay the night?"

She purses her lips and nods. "I could be persuaded. Though, this is getting to be a habit."

I run my hands down her back, giving her arse a gentle squeeze. She giggles. "Good habit or bad habit?"

"I have yet to decide."

"Just as well there's plenty of time."

All the time in the world.

17

OWEN

Mondays are the worst.

I wake with Ginny in my arms, and sigh at the thought of weeknights without her.

"Ginny," I say as I flick on the bedside light.

She stirs. "What time is it?"

"Four. I've got to get to work."

Her eyes flicker open. "Why are you waking me up?"

"I need to know. Will you stay the night?"

She closes her eyes again for a moment before frowning. "Owen, it's so important that you and Ava get time together."

"We are. She lives here now."

Ginny sighs. "*You* need time with her, Owen. Just you two. It's as important as the three of us spending time together."

"The weekends aren't enough."

She reaches for me, pulling me down and planting a kiss

on my lips. "I love you, but can we talk about this another time when it's not four in the morning?"

"I'm sorry. I just wanted another night with you."

"I just stayed three in a row." She lets out another sigh. "Please don't make this harder than it is."

I nod. "Sorry. I'll go to work. You get back to sleep."

She watches in silence as I pull my clothes on and turn off the light.

It's not until six, when the bread-making's done and I take a breather, that I realise I left the room without kissing her goodbye.

What an arse.

"I've gotta go for a second," I say to Mel.

"Ava's not up for an hour. Look. I made a special Ava cookie."

I turn. Mel's used my gingerbread cutters to make a shortbread girl. It's iced with a purple dress, and that touches my heart. "She'll love it."

"We've all got to do our bit to help her fit in, right?"

Ginny's words come back to me. I'm impatient to be with her, but she's right. Ava and I do need time together to get to know each other. We've barely scratched the surface. I may know her favourite colour, but what else about this little girl do I really understand? She doesn't talk about her former life, and she must remember the accident because she remembered me.

"It means a lot, Mel."

She shrugs. "Ava's dad's paying for it anyway."

Ginny's gone when I get back in the house. We didn't have an arrangement for this morning, and Ava will wake around seven and come and find me, just like she did last week.

Given that she could have gone home and gone back to sleep, I'll call her and grovel at a more appropriate time, maybe send her some flowers. I could kick myself for how I acted.

An hour later, as predicted, Ava's at the kitchen door.

"You ready for breakfast?" I ask.

"Where's Ginny?"

I bend, taking her hands in mine. "She's gone to her place. She needs to get changed and ready for work."

Ava's lower lip droops, and you'd think from her expression that she'd lost her favourite toy.

"We'll see her during the week. You and me need to get some groceries soon too, so maybe you could tell me what else you used to have for breakfast."

"Coco Pops."

"I'll add them to our list. That list is getting pretty big now, and I know you're sick of using my body wash in the bath."

She nods.

"Let's go and get something to eat."

———

GINNY'S PHONE'S off for most of the day while she's at work, and when I call I get her voicemail. I close my eyes at the sound of her voice.

"Hey, babe. I'm sorry about this morning. I was a bit of a dick, and I should have at least let you sleep. Call me later. I love you."

I hang up the phone and stare at it.

This situation is so foreign and yet it doesn't feel wrong. I'd rather have Ginny in my life and not staying nights than lose her altogether.

She hasn't returned my call by nine, and Ava's sound asleep.

Yawning, I look at the clock. I got used to Ginny staying a few nights, and falling asleep alone will be hard. How quickly things have changed.

I need to try and get some sleep. The whole "being up at four" thing is a grind, but I'm so proud of my little bakery. I worked my arse off to buy it, and it's all mine.

Hugging Ginny's pillow, I close my eyes.

"Owen?"

I open my eyes. It's dark.

"Ava?"

As I sit, I reach for the bedside lamp. She's standing beside the bed, her teddy-bear in one hand, her thumb in her mouth.

"Are you okay?"

She takes a step back and shakes her head.

"What's wrong?"

Her eyes fill with fear, as if she thinks she's going to be in trouble.

I slip out of bed and kneel in front of her. Stroking her hair gets me a small smile. "Are you going to tell me what's wrong?"

Her lower lip wobbles. "I wet the bed."

My heart melts. "Oh, honey, it's not your fault. Do you want me to sort it out?"

She nods.

"Tell you what. How about we get you changed and you come and hop into my bed?"

The clock tells me it's a little after one, and I have three hours before I need to get back up.

She nods again.

"Come on then."

Ava takes my hand, and I lead her back to her bedroom. I still have no idea what I'm doing, but I have to try for her, no matter how tired I am.

I open her top drawer. Ginny got her four more pairs of pyjamas, and I pull out the pink ones I know Ava likes. "Let me just grab you a new pair of knickers and we'll get you cleaned up."

"Mummy let me wear pull-ups."

I spin around. Ava hasn't spoken about either of her parents since she got here. Is this a good sign, or a bad sign?

"Really? You're so good at going to the toilet."

"Just for night-time."

I smile. "Okay. So tomorrow, we'll go and get some pull-ups for night. Would that be better?"

She grins, and I reach for her hand.

"Come on." I strip off her pyjamas, and run some warm water on a flannel. After I wipe her down, I grab a towel from the rail and dry her off. *Maybe I'm not so bad at this dad thing after all.*

When I've dressed her, she giggles as I pick her up and carry her to my room. Covering her with the duvet, I turn to go out the door.

"Owen? Where are you going?"

"I'm just going to strip the bed and throw the sheets in the wash with your clothes."

Her blue eyes, so much like Cara's, stare at me, and it hits me in the chest. Before Ginny, the woman I grew closest to was Cara Mitchell. She was the only married woman I ever slept with, and every time I look at her daughter, *our* daughter, I think I know why she chased me so hard. Maybe I was the solution to her problem.

I gave her everything she needed but I never knew.

"I'll be back in a minute." I give Ava what I hope is a reassuring smile and leave.

When I return, she's moved a little closer to my side of the bed, and she's still wide awake.

"Let's get some sleep." I yawn as I climb into bed beside her.

"Owen?"

"Yes?"

"Can I stay here?"

I roll to look at her, and I see hope in her face. "Here? You need to sleep in your bed tomorrow when it's clean."

She shakes her head. "No. Can I stay here at the bakery?"

My throat tightens as I realise she's asking if she's going to be shipped off somewhere else. She's four years old, and I haven't even stopped to tell her that she's living with me permanently.

"You live here now, sweetheart. This is your home. You can help me decorate your room. What's your favourite colour?"

"Purple."

I smile. "Then we paint it purple. I know you're scared, Ava. So am I sometimes."

"You are?"

"I've never looked after a little girl before. You have to

help me. Telling me about the pull-ups was a really good thing, because now I know how to make things better for you."

She bites down on her bottom lip. "Can I have a gingerbread man for breakfast?"

I go to sleep with a grin, giving her a promise that I'll make her a special gingerbread man when I wake.

We're getting there.

THE ALARM BEEPS AT FOUR, and I stumble out of bed.

Tugging on a pair of pants and a shirt, I head toward the door.

Ava.

Turning back, I switch the light back on and take a look. She's fast asleep, and it brings a smile to my face. She knows where I am when she wakes up, but she's not in the room she's getting used to. I'll have to come back and check on her.

Am I overthinking it?

This whole dad thing is not coming naturally, even if Ginny thinks I'm doing a good job of it. I'm second-guessing myself the whole way and now is no exception.

Maybe I shouldn't worry so much.

Ava turns up in the bakery kitchen a little before seven. The grin on her face makes me grin. The longer she's here, the more I see me in her.

"Good morning. Want some breakfast?"

Ava nods.

"Mel, I'm just going to go and sort Ava's breakfast out."

Mel nods. "Sweet as. Morning, Ava."

Ava waves. She's got Mel twisted around her little finger, and I need to get her out of here before she ends up with more cookies for her meal.

"Let's go find something to eat." I take her by the hand and lead her into the flat and toward the kitchen. "Toast with Marmite on it and a hot chocolate. Sound good?"

Ava nods.

"I don't even really know what you like. I've been making you what I like."

"I like Marmite. And hot chocolate."

I grin. "Well, that's a good start. But you can't live on Marmite and hot chocolate." I slip two slices of bread in the toaster. "I know you like spaghetti and meatballs. You like them so much that you lick your hands clean."

She giggles as she sits at the table.

"Anything else you really like?"

Ava nods again. "Lots."

"Nice. I'll fill the cupboards with lots, then."

I really can do this.

My phone buzzes on the table, and I pick it up.

Sorry. I left work early yesterday feeling gross and just woke up. I love you too.

Are you okay? Do you need anything?

I hate the thought of her being sick.

No. I'm staying home in bed today. I'll come and see you two when I'm feeling better.

I can ask Lily to look after Ava if you want me to come over.

I just need to get some sleep. I love that you care.

Okay. Love you.

This is why I need to convince her to move in. Knowing she's unwell and alone doesn't sit right with me. We need her, and she needs us.

I really have to work this out.

18

OWEN

Our grocery shop is overdue, and the list of things that Ava needs is getting longer. I hate shopping, but it's a necessity.

We drive the short distance from the bakery to the Four Square.

Reaching the door of the supermarket, I spot Mary Cuthbert.

"Ava." Mary walks out from behind the counter, and Ava runs into her arms.

Mary lifts her up, planting kisses on her cheek.

"I guess you two know one another." I laugh.

"Cara used to bring Ava in for a treat all the time. It's so good to see her. She's just like one of my *moko*." She smiles widely. "Is she living with you now?"

My jaw drops. "Did you know?"

Mary rolls her eyes. "I'm a big people watcher, Owen

Campbell. And apparently, I'm better at adding than you are."

I can't help but laugh. "It seems I was almost the last to know."

"Well, whatever the case, I'm so glad to see Ava." She turns to look at the girl. "It's lovely to see a big smile on your face. Do you like living with your father?"

Ava nods with enthusiasm. "He makes cookies."

"Yes, he does. And now you get to visit me again from time to time. That'll be nice, won't it?"

I grin. "Ava, we need to get some shopping. Are you going to help me put some things in the trolley?"

"Yes," she yells, clapping her hands.

"That's my girl. Come on." I say it without even thinking, and it gives me a warm fuzzy to think of her that way.

Ava wriggles down as Mary gives her another kiss on the cheek. "It's good to see you both. If you ever need a babysitter, Owen, give me a call."

"Thanks, Mary. I might just take you up on that sometime."

Grabbing a trolley, I start off down the aisle. I'm terrible at looking after myself at times, and there's no fresh food in the house right now.

Ava picks out the fruit she wants, and we move up and down the aisles, filling the trolley.

"What else do we need?"

"Pull-ups." Ava squeezes my hand.

I smile at her. "I'm glad I have you to remind me."

"Ava?"

I look up, and see Linda Green approaching. She runs the

local day care, and it suddenly occurs to me that Ava probably went there before her parents' death.

"Hey, Linda."

She smiles at me. "You're looking after Ava?"

Shit. I hadn't thought about people asking, or gossiping. I've never cared what others think before, but now I have Ginny and Ava to worry about.

"Linda." Ava wraps her arms around Linda's waist.

"Ava lives with me now."

Her eyes widen. "Seriously?" She strokes Ava's hair. "We've missed you."

"We haven't had much time to sort anything out, but I probably need to talk to you about her coming to day care. I haven't worked out what to do with her during the day while I'm working. At the moment, she's hanging out in the bakery."

Linda smiles. "We'd love to have her back. She was with us part-time five days a week, but we have full-time slots available. Just let me know."

Ava lets go of Linda and jumps up and down excitedly. It brings a smile to my face as I find one more thing that might help her get through all of this.

The pieces are starting to fall into place.

I UNPACK the groceries at home, Ava under my feet the whole time. She goes through the bags, looking for the things we bought for her. Not only did she get the fruit she wanted, but there's also yoghurt and potato chips.

"Do you want to go back to day care?"

Ava nods.

"Then we'll do it. I need someone to take care of you so you don't eat all the cookies."

She giggles, squeezing my hand.

"How about I talk to Linda in the morning, and we'll see how quickly we can get you back? I bet you have friends there that you miss."

Ava nods.

"It'll be time to go to school in a year or so, too. You'll be able to go with Ginny. She's a teacher."

"I love Ginny."

I grin. "So do I, Ava. So do I."

Ginny probably won't stay the night again until Friday, and that's three days away. I busy myself making dinner for Ava. It's nothing fancy—mashed potato and chicken nibbles, but where I used to eat out most nights, I'm quite enjoying cooking for the two of us. Or three, when Ginny's here.

Tonight's just like the first night she was here, as she's yawning by the end of dinner. I'm not as organised as I was that first night, though, and I carry her to her room still in her clothing.

"Should we put your pyjamas on?" I ask. "Guess I should get the pull-ups too."

Ava gives me a nod, her eyes closing and snapping awake as she fights sleep.

I grab the packet of pull-ups and pull one out. It seems pretty straightforward.

Ava lies on the bed as I pull her pants and knickers off, slipping the pull-up on.

"That was surprisingly easy."

She's already asleep by the time I pull up her pyjama pants, and she flops in my arms as I struggle with her pyjama top. With it buttoned up, I let her flop down in her bed. As I pull the blanket over her, I watch her. She's so beautiful. Even after everything, I have trouble believing she's mine.

Without warning, I have tears in my eyes. Tears for Ava losing her parents. Tears for me finding out the truth. Tears because I'm happier than I have been in years, and it's taken Ginny and Ava to do that. How have I lived my life without them?

My heart's so full that I know I could never return to the life I had before Ginny. I never realised just how much I needed the stability a good relationship could bring.

Although, until Adam and Lily were reunited, and Drew fell for Hayley, it's not like I had a lot of great examples in my life.

I lean over and plant a gentle kiss on Ava's forehead.

Rather than climb into an empty bed, I go back to the living room and turn on the television.

It's not long before I'm asleep just like Ava.

I RUB my neck as my phone alarm goes off. After the last time I fell asleep on the couch, I made sure I had a back-up alarm, and I get dressed and stumble out to the bakery kitchen, much to the bemusement of Mel. At least she didn't have to wake me by flicking water in my face.

"You look like shit."

"I fell asleep on the couch."

She laughs. "I guess I should be grateful that you turned up at all."

I poke my tongue out at her as I get to washing my hands to start the day.

The time passes quite quickly before Ava turns up in the doorway.

"Hey, pretty girl. Time for breakfast?" I smile.

"I thought you'd never ask." Mel grins.

I roll my eyes. "You, be quiet. Come on, Ava."

This time we've got Coco Pops, and her beloved hot chocolate with marshmallows. The food disappears in minutes, and I smile watching her.

"We'll go and see Linda today and get you back to day care."

Ava nods, chocolate milk running down her chin.

"Looking forward to seeing your friends?"

"I like the bakery, too."

I chuckle. "I know you do. At least, I know you like the cookies. Especially those gingerbread men. Am I right?"

She nods.

"Well, if Linda can look after you today, when you get home, I'm sure I can have something special waiting."

Ava climbs down from her chair and runs to my seat. She climbs onto my lap and wraps her arms around my neck. I give her a hug. "You're such a good girl. I'm so proud of you." I close my eyes as her cheek grazes mine.

Sometimes, I feel so in control. Other times, I still feel like this is way too much for me to deal with.

Either way, this is my life.

After breakfast, we drive down the road to the day care.

Linda greets us at the door. "Owen, Ava, it's so good to see you."

"I was thinking that Ava needs to get back to some normality."

She nods. "I'm not surprised to see you. We'd love to have her back. It's a hundred and fifty a week, and we're open from 7.30 a.m. to 6.00 p.m."

"Okay. That's fine."

"There are some forms to fill out, but I'll sort those out for you." Linda smiles. "Why don't you leave her here with us, and go get some work done? I'm sure we'll be fine."

Ava looks up at me.

"Do you want to stay here for a while?"

She pouts.

"What's wrong?"

"I don't have my bag," she whispers, wrapping herself around my leg.

Linda squats in front of us. "It's okay. I'm sure Owen can get you a new one if you need it. Want to come and play with your friends?"

Ava nods.

Linda holds out a hand. "Come on, then."

As Ava takes Linda's hand, Linda leans a little closer. "Go and ask Mary. She usually has some schoolbags. All she needs to bring is a change of clothing, and a hat for playing outside."

"Okay. Thank you."

I look down at Ava. It's a bit weird leaving her behind, but it's good for both of us, I guess. It'll be nice to focus on work without worrying about her, but at the same time I'll miss having her around.

"What time do I pick her up?"

"We're open until six, so between now and then. I'll sort out the invoice, and it'll be ready when you come and get her."

I nod. "Okay. Ava, be good and have fun."

She lets go of Linda's hand and I bend to hug her.

"Bye," she says.

When I get to the door, I turn. Ava's already surrounded by the other kids, no doubt excited to see her. And she's excited, her little face lit up with a big smile.

This is the right thing to do.

DESPITE SEEING HER SO HAPPY, I watch the clock and wait for closing time.

Ginny's not coming over tonight, so it'll just be me and Ava. As much as I hate that Ginny's not going to be with us, I'm looking forward to hearing about Ava's day.

"Go and get her." Mel rolls her eyes at me. It's a little after four. "You've looked at that clock about fifty times in the last five minutes."

"Thanks. It's her first day back, and—"

She smiles. "You don't have to explain it to me. She's your daughter."

"That's still sinking in."

Mel laughs, walking around the counter to slap me on the back. "You're doing well. It's obvious Ava adores you. Ginny, too."

I sigh. "I want us to all be together."

"You will be. Give Ginny time. Settling down with you is a crazy enough thing to do, even without taking the kid into account."

"I can always rely on you to bring me down to Earth." I laugh.

"Always, my friend."

I don't hang around any longer, heading toward the day care. Earlier today, Mary dug out the perfect bag from her stock. It's got some cartoon character on it I don't know, but she assures me Ava will recognise it. It's at home, ready for tomorrow.

Tomorrow.

The thought of dropping Ava here for a full day tomorrow leaves my stomach aching. Which is crazy. *It's good for both of us.* I repeat it over and over in my head.

I know that, but I don't want her to ever feel alone. Even surrounded by the other kids, she might miss me.

Her face lights up when I enter the building. It's all I need to see to know how Ava feels about seeing me.

"She's had such a good day." Linda follows Ava as she throws herself into my arms. I can't explain how good it feels to hold her again, even though I only saw her a few short hours ago.

"Did you?" I ask Ava.

"I played with my friends," she says.

"Want to come back tomorrow?"

She nods, and I don't know whether to feel happy or heartbroken.

"Come on. Let's go get a cookie and hot chocolate at home. I've got a surprise for you."

On the way out, Linda hands me an envelope. "Here's all the info you need and an invoice."

"Thanks. I'll get that paid as fast as possible."

She nods. "I know you will. See you tomorrow, Ava?"

My heart settles as Ava nestles in on my shoulder.

I hope she's always so easy to please.

19

GINNY

IT SHOULD BE THE EASIEST DECISION IN THE WORLD TO MOVE in with Owen, but it isn't.

Every day, he and Ava grow closer. As hands-on as he's become, there's still a distance between them I don't think he can see. It's almost like he thinks someone's going to swoop in and make everything better. He has to learn to be a father, and not just a caretaker.

But he's getting there.

Her attachment to me is all kinds of wonderful and hard. While I don't doubt Owen loves me, and he's opened up his life and his heart, there's still a lingering doubt over his ability to commit. But then again, he proves that wrong all the time.

I don't want to leave him hanging, but nor do I want to jump in too fast.

All I know is that I love both him and Ava.

They're the family I thought I'd never have.

When the bell rings at three, the kids disperse quickly. I sit at my desk and prepare the classwork for the following day, as I often do. It's the best time for it, when no one's here and it's quiet.

Until Owen, I enjoyed my own company better than being alone. Now, my mind wanders, thinking of him and the evening we have planned. It's Wednesday, and I'm going to have dinner with Owen and Ava.

I don't even notice Nathan entering the room until he sits on the corner of my desk.

"Ginny." His eyes immediately go to my cleavage. It makes me sick. It's the most overt he's been. "I thought we should talk about the conference I mentioned a while ago. I've got more details, and I'd like to book us both in to go. There'll be some valuable information we can use here."

Nodding, I adjust my top to make sure he can't see anything. "It's a good idea."

"To save money, we'll share a room. The school budget is so tight."

I freeze, staring at him. He's worded it so it doesn't sound like a proposition directly, but the way he's looking at me so intensely leaves me in no doubt as to what he means. "I'll pay for a room of my own."

He smiles. "You don't need to."

"I want to." My stomach rolls, nausea flooding through me.

His smile disappears. "It'd be a shame to turn down an opportunity like this."

"I'm not turning down the conference, but there's no need to share a room."

We stare at each other for a moment before he turns and leaves without a further word.

I'm confused. Did he just remove my chance of going to a conference that could benefit my career?

When he's gone, I lean over my wastepaper basket and dry heave.

What just happened?

I HEAD out toward my car. There are sprinkles of rain, and I turn my face to the sky to curse the dark clouds overhead. They don't help my mood.

"Are you okay?" Becky's just got to her car, and she looks at me with concern all over her face.

I don't even know what to say.

"I'm always here to talk if you need to. Owen—"

"It's nothing to do with Owen," I snap, but I don't mean to.

She frowns. "Okay. Sorry I asked."

"It's okay, Becky, and I'm sorry I snapped. It's just that—"

"If you're feeling better tomorrow, we'll talk." She starts her car and backs out of her park. I sigh as she disappears into the distance and open my car door.

Turning the key in the ignition, the engine splutters. That's it. It doesn't start. There's nothing but a sick noise, and I slam the steering wheel in exasperation. "Damn it."

The only thing I need now is Nathan Webster to show up and offer to help me. As it is, I don't know what to do about his proposition.

Grabbing my phone out of my bag, I call Owen. I'm stressed and tired, and I just need him.

"Ginny?"

"Hey. My car died in the car park at school. Is now a good time? Would you be able to come and pick me up?"

"Of course. You okay? You sound stressed."

"I'll be happier when you get here."

"No problem. I'll give Adam a call. He can take a look at the car."

"Thanks, Owen."

"Love you, Gin."

I smile. Knowing how special those words are coming from him, I can't help it.

"Love you too."

20

OWEN

There's something wrong.

Ginny hasn't said as much, but she's giving me one-word answers, and her head's turned to look out the window.

It's just not her.

We're halfway back to my place, and I'm taking my time as the rain is torrential. Twenty minutes ago, it was spitting. Now, the rain falls in large, heavy drops that pummel the roof of the car.

"What's wrong?"

She sighs. "I just have a lot going on, and I need to work out what to do about it."

"Is it us? Have I done something wrong?"

She turns her tear-stained face to me, her eyes filling with horror. "No. Owen. What we have is perfect."

"You're crying. Something's going on with you, and I need to know what it is so I can fix it."

Ginny shakes her head. "You can't fix it."

I place my hand on her knee. "I can try. If it makes you sad, it needs to be taken care of. I don't want those beautiful eyes full of tears." I smile. "There's still some time before I have to pick up Ava from day care, so let's get some time alone."

"Why do you always say the right things at the right time?" She says the words between sobs. I'm still none the wiser, but I'll be damned if I ever see her this upset again. I need to get to the bottom of this.

I pull into my driveway, and we run into the house. We'll both need a change of clothing after this. At least Ginny has some clothes at my place. I still have to go and get Ava from day care, but there's something I need to take care of first.

"Come here." I grab Ginny's arm and pull her toward the sofa. With her in my arms, she's protected, safe. There's nothing in the world that can beat me when I'm with her. "Tell me what's happened."

She nods.

And then she tells me.

***

SHE'S ON THE COUCH, wrapped in a blanket and holding the big mug of hot chocolate I just made her.

I pace the living room, anger making my blood boil at the thought of that man being anywhere near her. How many others have there been over the years? Ginny, *my* Ginny, being harassed. She's an angel.

"Owen, sit down."

I fist my hands and flex. "I'm so angry. I knew the day of Cara and Ryan's funeral something was up with your reaction to him, and I just thought it was because he was your boss. And then I let it go when you told me it was nothing."

"I'm sorry," she whispers.

Letting out a loud breath, I sit on the couch and take the cup from her hand, placing it on the table. "I'm sure you thought it would go away."

"I've lived here for three years. He's been here so long I thought people would believe him over me. Plus, today's the first day he's really tried something."

Reaching up, I stroke her face, pushing her hair behind her ear. "You've done wonders for the kids you've taught. I've seen that with Max. It counts for a lot, Ginny. The world needs soft-hearted people like you, even if there are monsters out there who will try to take advantage." Taking her hand in mine, I press my lips to it. "I've got to go and slay a monster."

Her eyes wide. "Owen."

"You're my girl, and no one pulls that shit on you."

"What are you going to do?"

I smile. "Pretty sure Mrs Webster will have something to say about this. She and I go way back."

Ginny's face blanches, and I don't need her to tell me what she's thinking.

"No, I didn't sleep with her. But a lot of people in this town are regular visitors to my bakery. Her included."

"Please don't hurt her."

I lean over, and give Ginny a lingering kiss. The easiest thing in the world would be to stay. This whole thing is screwing up the limited time we have alone together. But some things are more important. Taking care of this problem is a biggie.

"You're amazing. I hope I'm making you realise that. You're scared and hurt, and all you're worrying about is someone else's feelings." I kiss her again. "But let me tell you what I know. There is nothing in the world I won't do to protect you. That's what love is, and with you I finally worked that out."

Ginny flings her arms around my neck. "When we started this, I didn't know what would happen. I'm so glad I took the chance."

For a moment, I breathe her in. I never thought it was possible to love someone this much.

My whole life, I've been scarred. I'll never forget that moment as a twelve-year-old, not understanding why my dad was kissing someone else. He loved my mum, didn't he? It left me so confused for so long, but with Ginny there is no confusion.

She lets go, cupping my face and looking into my eyes. "You're everything to me, Owen."

I'm too choked up to speak at first. Everything I feel is in her eyes. "I feel the same way, sweetheart. It's not one of our nights, but I don't want you going home alone tonight. Stay here. I'm going to do what I can to protect you."

"I know," she whispers.

With a final kiss, I head towards the door, turning as I get there.

"I'll grab Ava on the way home. I love you, Ginny."

"Love you too."

I TAKE a deep breath before raising my hand to knock on Kelly Webster's door.

She's a regular customer, and a nice person. I hate to lay this on her, but if this has happened to anyone else, she needs to know. I have enough respect for her to tell her the truth.

The Websters never had any children, and maybe that's why I'm not so fazed by telling her. With Ava in my life, I can't imagine what a breakup with Ginny would mean to her. It's my job to protect her from anything like that.

I tap the door, and Kelly smiles as she opens it.

"Owen Campbell. What a pleasant surprise."

"I need to talk to you."

"Oh?" Her eyebrows dip in concern, and my stomach twists into a knot. But I'm determined to see this through. She needs to know. "Come in."

She leads me into their living room. It's a cosy little place, and there are pictures on the mantel of her and Nathan. If it wasn't for Ginny back home, I'd leave and let her live out the rest of her life without knowing. But I can't do that.

I sit on the couch where she indicates.

"Would you like a coffee? Tea?"

I shake my head. "Thank you, but I'd really just like to talk."

She sits beside me.

Taking a deep breath, I focus on her. "Well, it's like this. Ginny's been invited to a conference for special needs children after the work she's done with Max."

Kelly nods. "Nathan's been talking about it. Sounds like a big deal."

"It is. For Ginny, anyway." I swallow. "See, the thing is that Nathan's told Ginny he only wants to book one hotel room for the two of them."

Her expression tightens.

"I don't want to hurt you. Ginny's such a sweetheart. She's been uncomfortable for a while, but didn't want to rock the boat with the kids she looks after, and—"

She sighs. "I've heard rumours. Just didn't want to believe them. Let me deal with this."

"I'm so sorry, Kelly. I just need to do what I can to protect my girl."

Her lips twitch. "Never thought I'd see the day when you had a girl to protect. There are plenty of rumours about you, too."

"I wish I could put a stop to them."

She nods. "You're a good man. If people don't understand that, it's on them, not you."

The door opens, and Nathan Webster strolls in. He fixes his gaze on me.

"I'll see myself out. Kelly." I nod toward Nathan. "Nathan."

I leave the house with a smile on my face. There's no way I'd want to be in Nathan Webster's shoes right now. His wife has always come across as tough as nails.

Ginny's safety is my number-one priority, and now I know she'll be out of danger.

She's all that matters.

ON THE WAY HOME, I stop at day care to pick up Ava.

At the sight of me, she runs from the other side of the

room, launching herself into my arms. I hold her tight, kissing her temple. "Ready to go home, sweet pea?"

She nods.

"Did you have a good day?"

Linda walks toward me, a smile on her face. "We had a great day. She's doing so well, Owen. I'm sure that's all down to you and the great care you're taking of her."

"We're trying to take care of each other. Aren't we, Ava?"

Ava wraps her arms around my neck and squishes her face against mine.

"I think she's almost back to how she was before …"

I nod. "That's the goal. Make her a happy little girl who feels safe. No more crazy stuff. See you tomorrow."

Plucking her bag from the peg, I turn and walk us back out toward the car.

"Owen?" Ava says.

"Yes?"

"Can I have a gingerbread man when we get home?

Home. My heart warms at the word. "Sure thing. Although I think you need to cut back on how many you're eating. You might turn into a gingerbread man."

Ava giggles, and it fills my heart.

Things are coming right.

———

SLEEP DOESN'T COME EASY.

Despite my conversation with Kelly Webster, I still worry about Ginny. She's had concerns about her career with this. Could I have made things worse?

No. Worse would have been her feeling pressured enough to go to that conference and share a room with Nathan.

Whatever happens, she's got me.

Rolling over, I study her features. Despite the night light I bought her, Ava still prefers it if the hall light's on, and it means I have enough light to take in Ginny. She's so at peace now, far from the stress of earlier today.

I love her so much.

It's nearly two when I get out of bed and head to the kitchen. Baking soothes my soul, and if I can't sleep, I might as well try and tire myself out.

On the bench is a bag of gluten-free flour. I bought it to experiment and try some new recipes. If Ginny needs it, there'll be other people who do, surely. Maybe the first time I tried selling it, it was ahead of the trend. Regardless, I'll make something for her.

Measuring out the ingredients, I tip my dough onto the floured board I bought for the occasion. I don't know how this will turn out, but it'll be worth it for the look on her face.

"What are you doing?" Ginny's voice comes from behind me.

"Making gluten-free bread." I turn to look at her as she steps into the room.

She runs her fingers through her long, brown hair. "It's two in the morning."

"I couldn't sleep. This is what I do when I can't sleep." Kneading the dough, I shape it under my hands.

She slips her arms around my waist and kisses my shoulder. "Come back to bed. Why can't you sleep? What's wrong?"

I heave a breath. "Everything. Nothing."

"What do you mean?"

"I'm worried that I've made things worse for you with the way I handled Nathan. And I worry about Ava. What am I doing, Ginny? What happens if I do something wrong?"

She lets go of me and moves to my side. I turn my head to look at her.

"How do you think other parents work it out? Parenting is trial and error. You're trying your best for that little girl, and you're doing an amazing job. Stop second-guessing yourself."

I sigh. "I can't help it."

"And as for me, I'm just glad I told you about it."

"I can't believe you hadn't told anyone here. Especially me."

She runs her hand down my back. "He didn't make any real move until he suggested the shared motel room. Oh, there was innuendo, and sometimes the way he looked at me made me uncomfortable. But I doubted myself. And you did nothing wrong. You took care of me."

I let go of the bread and turn to her. My hands are caked with gluten-free flour, but she takes them in hers.

"I love you, Owen. Once I thought maybe this whole Nathan thing was me imagining things, and I thought about leaving town just to get away from the situation. But nothing would drag me from this place now. Not with you and now Ava to love."

Cupping her face, I press my lips to hers. Her mouth opens a little, enough for me to run my tongue over her own. I lose it when her breathing quickens. "Maybe we should go back to bed."

She shakes her head. "You've got bread to finish."

"I'll leave it to rise and bake it in the morning." I drop my hands, and smile at the spots of flour on her cheeks. "Come here."

Pulling her in front of me, I pick up her hands and place them on the bread.

"What are you doing?" She laughs.

"You can finish kneading the bread."

She squeezes the dough, and I slip my hands between hers and show her what to do.

"Did you always want to be a baker?" she asks.

"Always. Baking was something Mum and I used to do together, and I loved every second of it." I pause. Mum hasn't done any baking for a long time. I doubt she'll do any more. "I loved being able to use my hands, and it wasn't just about the food. It was about the art."

I nuzzle Ginny's neck as she keeps kneading. Placing my hands on her hips, I press myself against her.

"How much is too much?" she asks.

"Never enough," I murmur, having lost interest in the bread. I'm far more interested in her skin.

"Owen." She laughs.

"It's fine." I reach around her and shape the dough into a loaf, placing it on a nearby tray.

"So that'll be ready to go in the morning?"

"It doesn't need that much time, but once I go back to bed with you, I'm not getting up again."

She slips her arms around my neck. "Thank you."

"What for?"

"For baking me bread. For loving me the way I love you."

"You know, that offer is always open for you to move in."

Ginny pulls me in for a kiss. "Soon," she whispers.

"Better be soon. You're busting my balls when you're not here."

She giggles.

We leave a trail of flour all the way back to the bedroom, and I don't care in the slightest.

I only wish she'd stay every night.

21

GINNY

Jessica Turfrey's waiting for me in my classroom when Owen drops me off in the morning. She's the deputy principal, and my stomach clenches at the sight of her.

"Ginny." She smiles.

"Hi, Jessica. How's it going?"

She clasps her hands together. "Nathan Webster resigned last night. I'll be the acting principal."

I nod, and wonder how much she knows.

"Becky Lane is going to be acting deputy principal until the board makes its appointments, but I'm certain they'll take my recommendations with everything being such short notice. So, with that in mind, I wondered if you were interested in the role of senior school team leader."

My stomach flips. "Me?"

"Everyone loves you, Ginny." She takes a big breath. "I had a call from Kelly Webster last night telling me what happened. For years, there have been whispers about

Nathan, and there was something not quite right, but there wasn't any proof."

I burst into tears. Owen believes in me. He never once questioned my story, and he's always on my side. Maybe I didn't give anyone else enough credit.

"Oh no." Jessica slips her arms around me, and I cry on her shoulder.

"I didn't know if anyone would believe me."

She gapes. "Why wouldn't we?"

"He's been here for so long, and I didn't know if it'd be taken seriously."

Jessica smiles. "Sounds to me like you've got a good man who went into battle for you. And I'm sorry you didn't feel like you could come to me. I would have listened."

"Thank you."

"That conference is yours, too. You're the perfect person to send to it. The work you've done here is fantastic, given our lack of resources. We'll catch up later in the day about the new position."

I nod.

And I can't wait to get home to Owen and Ava tonight.

***

ADAM PICKS me up after work.

"I'll take you to the garage. Your car's there, ready and waiting." He smiles.

"What was wrong with it?"

"Starter motor was buggered. I replaced it."

"What do I owe you?"

He chuckles. "Nothing."

"I can't pay you nothing for repairing my car."

"You're family, Ginny. Besides, what you're doing with Owen and Ava—I'm so grateful."

Tears well in my eyes. "I'm not doing anything special."

"You turned my brother's life around. And my niece has the stability she needs, thanks in part to you."

We travel the rest of the distance in silence, and when we stop outside the garage, he turns to me. "Here we are."

"Thank you, Adam."

"You're very welcome. I'm glad it was something simple."

"Me too."

Owen's cooking dinner when I get to his place. The smell of chicken fills the flat.

I'm tired from our early baking session, and weepy over the circumstances of my promotion. But I'm happy, and where I need to be.

Ava leaps up from the floor and wraps her arms around my waist. I hold her tight. Sometimes she wants me to carry her, and I do it even though it hurts. My body doesn't always behave when I want it to.

"Hey, sweetheart. Did you have a good day?" I ask her.

"I went to day care."

"I know you did. What did you do there?" Making my way to the couch, I sit down and she jumps up beside me.

"We made cookies."

"Did you?"

"I brought you one home." She plucks a little package from the coffee table, and I smile at the wrapping. It's all tied up in a pink bow.

"Thank you."

"Eat it. It's yummy."

I open it up, and it's a shortbread biscuit. It's round, and iced with a smiley face.

"She brought one for me too. I gave it an eight out of ten." Owen walks into the living room and stands behind the couch. I raise my face for him to lean over and kiss.

"Eight? That's generous coming from you."

"Well, maybe a six for the cookie, but Ava got points for bringing us both one home."

I laugh. "Maybe you can make some shortbread and show them how it's done."

"How was your day?" he asks.

"Nathan resigned. And after the dust settled, I got a promotion."

He grins, leaping over the couch—much to Ava's delight—and pulling me into his arms. "Then this is an extra special day."

"I still feel weird about it, and I feel like Nathan got away from any consequences by resigning, but it is good. I'm the team leader for the senior school."

"I'm so proud of you. And don't worry about Nathan. I'm sure Kelly will make him suffer, possibly forever, for it."

"You don't think it'll break them up?"

He shrugs. "I don't know. But either way, he's the one who ends up second best in this."

"Thank you for believing me."

"I'll always believe you."

Ava leans over, placing her weight on my pelvis. I suck in a breath at the pain.

"Eat your cookie," she says.

I grab her under her arms and pull her into a hug, relieving the pressure. "I'll eat it just for you."

"Are you sure you should?" Owen asks.

"It's just one cookie. I'll be fine."

Even if it's not, I'll do it for Ava.

I LOVE BEING HERE.

I'm the one holding out on the three of us being together, but right now this is where I need to be. There's so much we need to talk about when we do move in together. I'm dreading it.

But for the moment, when we've put Ava to bed and snuggled on the couch for a while, he takes me to his bed and all is right with the world.

He touches me gently, his hands caressing my body as he works his way down.

Even though I know it's coming, I still gasp as his tongue rolls over my clit. He knows I can't do this fast and hard, but he never asks why. He just gives me what I need.

This is why my heart belongs to Owen Campbell.

No one can tell me he's any different to this. He's the Owen I know and love.

I relax as he licks me, touches me, moans. Closing my eyes, I lose myself in the sensation, in Owen's attentions.

And he does pay attention to every little thing.

My body jerks as I come, the gentle build giving way to a whole-body experience.

"I can't wait any longer."

I open my eyes to see him over me, reaching for the condom. Running my hands over his chest, I hook my arms around his neck.

"Me either. I need you inside me."

When the condom's on, he slides slowly in.

"You feel so good. We could do this every night, you know."

"I know," I whisper.

We move together, and I fight the urge to close my eyes again, instead drowning in the love written all over his face. My heart's bonded with his, and it'll stay that way. I'm sure of it.

He presses in a little too deep, and I grip his biceps.

"Sorry. It's hard to hold back, but I don't want to hurt you."

I nod. "I know. It's okay."

"I love you, Ginny." His goofy smile shows what's in his heart. I never have to second-guess his feelings.

"I love you too."

He groans, stilling over me. Missionary has become my thing after other positions being too painful in the past. Yet, he just accepts it, and does whatever it takes to make me happy.

When he rolls to my side, I snuggle into his arms.

"What do you think about having children?"

I swallow. "I love kids. They're why I became a teacher."

"Drew and Hayley want a rugby union team's worth."

I laugh. "Fifteen?"

"I want a lot, but maybe not that much. I'll settle for a baker's dozen. About the same as a rugby league team."

My heart hurts. "*Thirteen*. You want that many children?"

"Not really, but it would be nice to have one or two. I've been thinking a lot since Ava moved in, and it upsets me that she's alone. I mean, can you imagine how much she'd love a brother or sister?"

I know more than ever that he's changed now. The Owen Becky knew would never have spoken about having children. I'm not taking credit for it. He's been through a lot these past couple of months, but this is just another example of the Owen I love.

What hurts is that I don't know if I can be the one to give him what he wants.

22

OWEN

Over the next month we fall into a routine.

Ginny still stays with us over the weekends. She and Ava grow closer, and I love seeing the two of them together. It just cements her place in our little family.

I just want her to stay.

"Mum wants us to come over for dinner on Saturday," Ginny says. It's been two months since I met her brother, and I'm more than ready to meet the rest of the family. We've tried to organise something a few times, but as it turns out, it's not so easy to get all the Robinsons in one place at one time.

"Sounds good. Does she need us to bring anything? I can bake a dessert."

She grins. "Sounds wonderful."

"Do they not eat gluten either? I'll make it gluten free, but I'm just curious."

She shakes her head. "No, they're all fine."

"What is it that makes you avoid it?" I flick a lock of her hair behind her ear. We're vegged out in front of the television while Ava plays in her room.

Ginny takes a deep breath. "Well—"

"Owen, Ginny, look at this." Ava comes running in with her colouring book. I've discovered she loves drawing and colouring, and bought her all kinds of pens and paper.

"What is it?"

She beams, holding her book up. "It's a family. I coloured this in. There's Ginny, you, and me." Ava frowns. "There's a dog too. I think that must be Lucky."

I grab her around the waist, and she squeals as I pull her onto my lap. "That's a very nice picture. You're pretty good at staying in the lines."

When I look over at Ginny, she has tears in her eyes. "That's us?" Her voice cracks.

"Yep." Ava leans into me, and I kiss her temple.

"Oh, honey, it's beautiful."

Ava leaps off me and runs back toward her room. "Where are you going?" I call.

"More pictures."

I shift my gaze to Ginny, and pull her into my arms. "You okay?"

"She thinks of us all as a family."

"Because we are."

The conflict's all over her face. "I can't step in as her mother."

"I think it's too late for that. And I don't think that either of us are stepping in as her parents. Cara and Ryan will always be her parents. But she loves both of us."

Ginny swallows hard as she looks at me, and the tears roll down her cheeks.

"Come here." I hug her, and she leans her head to rest on my shoulder.

Whether she wants it or not, she's it, as far as Ava's concerned.

And I think she makes an amazing mother.

ON SATURDAY, we make the drive to Carlstown to have dinner with Ginny's family.

Kyle stands in the doorway, smiling as we pull into the backyard. I present him with a plastic bag. "For you and Jordan."

His jaw drops. "No. You didn't." He opens the bag. "Holy shit, you did."

"Hope that's enough."

"I told him not to give you any," Ginny says. "It's setting a dangerous precedent."

"What's a dangerous precedent?" Another tall, well-built guy comes up behind Kyle.

"Owen, this is Jordan. Jordan, this is Owen."

"Hey, dude," Jordan says.

"Check this out. Owen brought us a bag of pies. You know those amazing ones we get in Copper Creek?"

His grin widens. "Awesome. They're worth the drive."

"Thanks." I laugh.

"Come in. Mum and Dad are gonna love meeting you."

I take a step into the kitchen. The air's full of the aroma of roasting lamb, and my mouth waters at the scent.

"This must be Owen." A woman I can only assume is Ginny's mother comes walking toward me. She's a lot like Ginny, only older.

"It is." I grin.

"I'm Adele." She points to a man sitting at the table. "And this is Lloyd, Ginny's Dad."

"It's so good to meet both of you. I made a cheesecake for dessert," I say, and she takes the container from me.

"Thank you." She beams.

"Dad, Owen brought some of those pies Jordan and I told you about," Kyle says.

Lloyd grins. "Sounds great." He gets up and walks toward me, extending his hand. He claps me on the back as we shake hands. "It's great to finally meet you. Ginny's told us all about you, and your little girl."

"Here she is," Ginny says.

Ginny's mother claps her hands to her cheeks. "Oh, Ginny, she's just as beautiful as you told me she was."

"Ava, this is my mum and dad." Ginny takes another step forward.

I've been here two minutes, and already I feel comfortable.

I think Ava and I are going to like this place just fine.

DINNER IS AMAZING.

It reminds me a lot of the family dinners we used to have before Adam went away and Mum got sick. The Robinsons are obviously a close family when they actually get together, and Ava doesn't know who to look at, they're all so busy fussing over her.

"I'm glad you've found a good boyfriend after the awful one you had last time."

"Mum," Ginny says.

"Piece of shit," Jordan mutters.

I turn to Ginny.

"Not in front of Ava." She grits her teeth.

"Shit, sorry," Kyle says, and Ginny rolls her eyes.

"Ava, don't listen to either of them. They're so bad at saying naughty words," Ginny says.

Ava snuggles in against me.

"Owen, you need to marry my sister. These pies are the best ever." Kyle's already eaten his dinner, and is now getting stuck into the pies. He takes another bite, and I chuckle.

"I'll never understand how you can interrogate him like you're so suspicious of his intentions, and the next you're wanting to marry me off for a meat pie." Ginny laughs.

"Nah, he's a good dude. Ava's pretty cool too." Kyle winks at Ava. "We just like giving him a hard time because he's with you."

"Never could have guessed." I grin.

Ava tugs on my arm, and I lean over so she can whisper in my ear. "Are there any gingerbread men?" She tries to whisper, but it comes out so loud everyone can hear it.

I shake my head. "Not here. Maybe when we get home. There's a cheesecake for dessert though, so you can have a piece of that."

She frowns. "But I want a gingerbread man."

"I'm sorry, Ava, but I don't have any."

She lets go of an almighty wail, and tears roll down her

cheeks. In the past month, she's been so good. This is the first time she's played up, and of course, it has to be while I'm trying to impress Ginny's family.

"Ava, come on."

"I want to go home." She sniffs, and I pull her onto my lap.

"What's going on?" I stroke her hair.

"She's tired," Ginny says. "Do you want to go for a nap, Ava?"

Ava rubs her eyes, and snuggles into my chest.

"Do you know what? You can sleep in my old room if you want. I'll sit with you until you go to sleep, and then we can wake you up when it's time to go home." Ginny gets up and walks around the table, squatting beside me. "Come on, munchkin. Today's been a big, exciting day for you."

Ava takes Ginny's hand, and I watch helplessly as they leave the room.

"She's so good with kids," Jordan says.

"She's been amazing with Ava. I don't know what I would have done without her these past few weeks." I look at Adele. "I only discovered Ava was my daughter a few months ago when she came to live with me. It's a big thing to adjust to, but Ginny's been fantastic."

Adele's eyes mist over. "Ginny always wanted children. She was so disappointed to find out there wasn't much chance she'd ever have them. It does my heart good to see her with your daughter."

I blink in rapid succession, trying to take in what she's just told me. But there's no way I can hide from her that what she's just said has come as a surprise to me.

"Good one, Mum," Jordan grumbles.

"Oh, Owen, I'm sorry. I just assumed Ginny had told you. I've got such a big mouth sometimes."

I lick my lips. "It's okay. I'm sure she'll tell me when she's ready."

Ginny appears in the doorway, a big smile on her face. "She was out like a light. Remember when we came here shopping, and she fell asleep in the car on the way home? I think the travel just wears her out."

"It would explain why she was so cranky. She's never got upset like that before."

Ginny shakes her head, making her way back to the table. "No, it's not like her, but I guess we're still learning about each other."

I meet her gaze. "We sure are."

***

WE FEEL like our own little family back home.

Ava's back to her usual self after a nap, and she's awake the whole car ride home, but a story from Ginny and she falls asleep.

I watch from the doorway. My whole world is in this room, and it's not tainted by my discovery. It disappoints me Ginny hasn't confided in me yet, but I guess she will in time.

All I know is that no matter what, it's her I want.

I know the thought of her and Ava getting too attached to one another scares her, but it's a magical thing to watch. And deep down I love that I can give Ginny what she wants, even if she can't have children with me.

In the absence of Ava's biological mother, she's got the

next best thing. And Ginny couldn't love Ava any more than she does.

Sometimes at night, I lie awake and think of Cara. It's too late to tell her how hurt and angry I am at her for not telling me I had a daughter, for this to have been sprung on me without any prior knowledge. It's turned my life upside down, but in such a short space of time I've been left not wanting things to be any other way.

It also hurts that Cara will never see her little girl grow up.

Somehow, I have to guide Ava through that, work out how to help her become a young woman without screwing things up.

I just hope that Ginny's by my side the whole way.

23

***

OWEN

TODAY'S THE DAY OF ADAM AND LILY'S LITTLE CEREMONY, THE one they've been planning since Rose was born.

It's a Māori tradition to bury the placenta and umbilical cord of your baby. It symbolises the relationship between the child and the place of their birth, but for Adam and Lily, it's also about finding each other again and forming their family. Adam bought this house with the garage when he came home, and it's their first family home. One they plan on being in for a long time.

Doing this seems so appropriate for their situation.

Knowing what they've been through has helped give me confidence that I can do the family thing too. And so far, so good.

Ginny's in the car with me on the way to Adam and Lily's, with Ava in the back seat. A little voice sings the *Dora the Explorer* theme at the top of her lungs. It was the last thing Ava saw before we got in the car.

Ava's been with me for four months, and in that time, her self-confidence has grown. She rarely speaks about her parents, but sometimes she slips them into the conversation. Usually when I'm saying no to something Cara apparently used to say yes to. If she's testing boundaries now, I hate to think of what she'll be like as a teenager.

"We're here." I pull up outside. The driveway's full, with Drew's car, Corey's truck, and … "Huh."

"What's up?" Ginny asks.

"That's Dad's car. Hell must have frozen over."

She nudges me with her elbow. "That's not nice."

"Maybe not, but it's true." I lean over and peck her on the lips. "Let's go do this. Ava, are you excited to see Max and Rose?"

"And Luckyyyyyyyy," she yells.

"Even Lucky."

She's so noisy, but it's music to my ears.

Ava's happy.

We all get out of the car, and I grab the bread from the back seat. We're having a barbecue for dinner, and that's my contribution.

Ava holds out her hands to both of us, and Ginny and I take one each, swinging our arms as we walk in the gate. As we reach the deck, I come to a complete stop.

"What are you doing?" Ginny laughs.

I nod toward the chairs. "Look."

On the deck and overlooking proceedings are my parents. Both of them.

Mum sits in a chair, a shawl around her shoulders. She's looking more frail than last time I saw her, but that was in the comfort of her home and not sitting outside in a warm breeze.

Lily walks toward us, smiling widely. "Hi, guys. Ava, Max is just inside playing games with Corey if you want to go and see them. Your grandad's in there too."

"I'll take you." Adam comes up behind her, and Ava follows him in.

"What's going on? Mum's here?"

Lily nods. "I called them. Today is a special day, and I kept hearing how she's going downhill. What she did to Adam and me was unforgivable, but we need to set that aside for the kids. She's likely to have only a few months left, and they should be able to get to know her."

Ginny grasps Lily's arm. "That's a lovely gesture."

"It's not easy. We'll be planning our wedding soon, as Adam's therapy isn't so frequent now, and we'll have a bit more money to spend on it. So, I figured it was time to try and mend a bridge."

"That's great," Ginny says.

"Honestly, Ginny, I just want to marry him and be done with it. But we deserve something special."

I slip my arm around Ginny's waist. "Yeah, you both do. And I need an excuse to make another amazing cake."

She laughs. "Yes. Now, go and see your mother and keep her entertained so I don't have to talk to her. Once our ceremony's over, she'll move inside and spend some time with the kids."

"That's such a great idea. Are they coming out here for the ceremony?"

Lily nods. "I think it'll be a bit boring for them, but it won't take long, and then they can go back to playing."

"Sounds like a plan."

I mount the steps to the deck, heading toward my mother.

"Hey, Mum." I lean over and plant a kiss on her forehead before taking the seat next to her.

"Owen."

"It's good to see you here."

She nods. "Lily called. I was surprised, but I appreciate the gesture."

"We're only missing James."

Mum nods. "He said he'd come, and Lily arranged the weekend around his schedule. But I think he's struggling a bit to prepare for his exams, and he wanted to stay in Auckland."

"That's a shame."

"He's a good boy. You all are." She sighs. "I know they don't really want me here, but I'm grateful to see my grandchildren. Max is such a delight." Her eyes grow misty. "I'm only sorry I didn't take the time to get to know him years ago. I'll always regret it."

"Have you told Lily and Adam that?"

She shakes her head.

"God, Mum, you're so stubborn."

Mum smiles. "It's a trait more than one of my sons has inherited."

I grin. "I think you're right there."

"You and Ginny make a beautiful couple." Her change of subject catches me by surprise. "Marry that girl, Owen. If I've learned one thing, it's that life's too short for regrets. No one knows that more than I do right now."

I lean over, and wrap my arms around her frail body. "I will. If she'll agree."

"It's very clear how much she loves you. And that little girl needs both of you."

"I know," I whisper.

"I'm glad you found someone. Now to sort out Corey."

Letting go, I look into her eyes. "No one can sort Corey out, Mum."

She laughs. "Maybe you're right. He's the most stubborn of all my boys. I'm so proud of all of you."

It's been a long time since I've seen her like this. Maybe it's because she's resigned to her fate, but I'm so glad she's not become more bitter and twisted than ever before. It's been so many years since we've been together like this, back before Adam left. And now, our family's become so much bigger.

If only we could be like this all the time.

It's hard to think of a world without my mother. Even when we disagree, and her nasty streak comes out, she is always a stable in our lives. My brothers and I all always knew if we ever needed defending, she'd be our staunchest advocate. And even though we're all grown up now, someone having that unwavering faith in us is something we've all appreciated at different times during our lives.

Mum's no angel, but she loves us. Even if she has a funny way of showing it at times.

Ginny sits on my other side, and I reach for her hand, lifting it to my lips. She looks past me.

"Hi, Ginny," Mum says.

"Hi, Mrs Campbell."

Mum smiles. "Please, call me Joanna."

Seeing them interact is wonderful. We haven't spent a lot of time with both her and my father. Mum's resting a lot these days.

"Love you." I mouth it, and Ginny leans in, resting her head on my shoulder.

"Hey, you two." We turn as Hayley walks out of the house behind us. I grin at the sight of her.

"Here." I stand, offering her my chair.

She shakes her head. "I'm the size of a house. I doubt my fat arse would fit in that seat."

"There's nothing wrong with your arse." Drew stands in the doorway, two beers in hand. "Take the chair."

"Okay, Okay. I'll just waddle over here." Hayley winks as she makes her way past Ginny and sits beside Mum.

"Want a beer?" I ask Ginny.

She shakes her head. "Go and drink with your brother. I'll catch up with Hayley."

Drew holds a bottle out to me as I approach.

"How much longer?" I ask, nodding toward Hayley.

"Hopefully about five weeks. Hayley would be glad if it was over tomorrow, but if we can get her to thirty-seven weeks, we should be clear of any trouble."

I smile. "I'm so happy for you guys. It's what you always wanted."

"When you know, you know. I'm really proud of you still being with Ginny."

Nodding, I take a sip of my beer. "Like you said. When you know, you know."

Adam's palm lands on my back. "It's time to go outside."

"On our way." Drew holds up his beer bottle, and I clink mine against it. "To family."

"To family." I grin as he grips my shoulder. "Everything is so good right now."

"It sure is."

MUM'S not steady on her feet, so we gather around her on the deck to watch.

"We had the land blessed this morning," Adam announces. "So we'll get this done pretty quickly and onto dinner."

Mum looks up at me when I rest my hand on her shoulder, and I smile.

Ava runs to my side as the kids come out, and tugs on my other hand. I look down to see her with her arms up. Gathering her onto my hip, I lean my head against hers.

The flax basket containing Rose's placenta is carried out by Lily. With Adam by her side, they both walk to the hole in the ground and gently place it in.

The tree's planted over the top, and Adam, Lily, and Max kneel to push the dirt around the base of it. I laugh at the sight of Rose beside Max, patting down the earth and holding her dirty hands up in delight. For Adam and Lily, the symbolism is everything. This home was their new start, their chance to set aside the years apart and have their family the way they always planned.

When I think about all the years they lost, it makes me all the more determined to get things right with Ginny the first time around.

I shift my gaze to her, and she gives me a loving smile. I'd like to think that maybe one day this will be us. That one day we'll need a bigger house for our family. I'll give her the family she wants, one way or another. If we can't have babies, maybe we can adopt. I don't know.

What I do know is that I want my future to be with her.

AFTER DINNER, with Mum having gone home and everyone else inside, Ginny and I sit on Adam's deck and watch the sun going down.

Today's been amazing for so many reasons. My family's united in a way I thought would never happen again, and Ginny and Ava are a massive part of that.

"Thank you for bringing me," Ginny says. We're on the edge of the deck, swinging our feet over the side. Ava's watching a Disney princess movie inside with Hayley. I have no clue which one, but I guess at some point I need to work all that out.

"You're part of the family. I'm sorry James couldn't make it. Exam time must be pretty hardcore."

"It is," Ginny says.

"You'll get to meet him either when he's here for the holidays, or we can take a trip to Auckland."

"Going to Auckland would be great once the babies are born. Drew and Hayley are going to need all the help they can get."

I run my fingers through her hair. "They will. I can't imagine how crazy their life is about to become."

The light is fading, but I don't miss her reaction. I've put my foot in it, and I know why, thanks to her mother. I don't want to confront her with something she hasn't confided in me, but the last thing I want to do is to hurt her.

Pulling her closer, I wrap my arms around her. "Our life is crazy enough now that we have Ava."

I close my eyes as she rests her head on my shoulder. I'm not sure what her reaction to that is, but I'll do whatever it takes to protect her.

"Ava's amazing," she whispers. "So are you."

"Must run in the family." I chuckle, letting her go so I can look her in the face.

"Must do." The corners of her mouth turn up. If I didn't know what I do, I wouldn't think she was fazed by what I'd said.

"Move in with us."

She shakes her head.

"Why not?"

"I'll tell you when it's time."

I sigh. "Ava and I are doing really well. We've got our routine sorted. Now all we need is you."

She raises her hand, running her fingers down my temple. "Soon. You're nearly there."

"Nearly where?"

"You'll see."

24

DREW

At thirty-five weeks pregnant, Hayley's over it.

I can't blame her. Pregnancy is tiring enough. With twins, she's tired and bloated and just wants it to be over. But our babies need a bit longer. Chances are they won't go the distance to forty weeks, but if we can get to thirty-seven we'll be fine.

Now, more than ever, my wife gets whatever she wants, and what she wanted this weekend was to see her mother.

Once Sonya realised that she couldn't control her daughter's life, and we were married, she's been a lot easier to get along with. Hayley's closer to her than ever, which is going to come in real handy once the babies are born.

My mother's declining health makes it unlikely she'll be involved much.

We arrived last night, spending the night at Hayley's parents'. Today, we'll catch up with James, and Hayley's looking forward to spending more time with her mum before we go home tomorrow.

I wake to her curled around me. As much as she can, anyway, with the bulk of our two babies in front of her. When she's this close, I can feel them move inside her. It's not like I haven't felt babies move before, but the thought that they're half mine fills me with wonder.

"Morning," she murmurs.

"Good morning, beautiful."

She laughs. "Bloated, more like."

"Still beautiful. Always beautiful." I kiss her softly. "Want some breakfast?"

"Yes, but I don't want to get out of bed."

Laughing, I stroke her cheek. "You don't have to. I'll bring some up for you."

When I reach the kitchen, David and Sonya are up and eating.

"Where's Hayley?" Sonya asks.

"She's having a lie-in. I was going to grab something and take it to her."

Sonya nods. "I'll sort her out some juice and toast."

"Sounds good. She's been a bit miserable lately. The pregnancy's been really hard on her. I'll be glad when our babies are here, and I can help give her a break."

I sit at the table while Sonya disappears to make something for Hayley.

"What are your plans for the day?" David asks.

"We thought we might go and visit James. We haven't caught up with him for ages, and then we'll come back and hang out here. Hayley really just wanted to be home for a bit."

He smiles. "I'm glad she and Sonya have repaired their relationship."

"Me too."

"How's your mother?"

I shrug. "Up and down. The cancer's back, and invasive. It's hard to say how long she's got left, but she's determined to live out whatever time she has at home."

"No treatment?"

"It's so much worse this time. I've just been hoping she lives long enough to see my children."

David nods. "Please pass on our regards next time you see her."

"Of course. She enjoyed the time you all spent together during the wedding. I think it was a good distraction."

Sonya places a tray on the table in front of me. "There's enough for both of you."

I look up to my smiling mother-in-law. Our relationship is a far cry from what it was when we started, and I'm so thankful that Sonya's now so supportive of us.

"If you need anything else, Drew, let me know." Sonya pats me on the shoulder.

"I will. Thanks."

***

HAYLEY EATS SLOWLY, and I can see from her tired eyes how exhausted she is. When she's finished, I move the tray to the bedside cabinet.

"You didn't sleep well," I say.

"I never sleep well these days." She lets out a half-hearted laugh.

"Not long to go now, princess."

Hayley sighs. "I know, but it's not going fast enough."

"I'm going to go and see James. Are you coming with me?"

She pouts. "I really want to, but I'm so tired."

I lean over and plant a kiss on her forehead. "It's okay. I'll give James your love."

"Thank you."

For a moment, I watch as she closes her eyes. It makes me a little uneasy to leave her here, but I'm no use if she needs the rest.

"I won't be long," I whisper.

She murmurs something, and I smile. Hayley can fall asleep in thirty seconds sometimes, and today looks like one of those days.

Sonya's in the living room when I go downstairs. She looks up at me and smiles.

"Hayley's tired, so she's having a nap."

She nods. "I know it's not that far to Hamilton, but the trip would have worn her out."

"All we need to do is get two more weeks to be safe."

Sonya smiles. "Let's hope the time passes quickly for you both. I'll check up on her while you're out."

"Thanks, Sonya."

It's another hour to drive from their rural property into the city. James is living in student accommodation near the university. I tried calling him on the way and got his voice-mail. Maybe I should have phoned him last night, but this was a spur-of-the-moment trip, and right now, I'd do anything to keep Hayley happy.

It hurts to see her exhausted, and I'd take some of the

load off if I could.

Seeing the students hanging around in the foyer brings back memories. I started off here before moving to Hamilton when I began work at the hospital. It seems like so long ago, but it really wasn't.

I know something's wrong the minute James opens the door.

His dark hair is a greasy mess, like he hasn't washed it in at least a week. He's got food stains on his T-shirt, and his hangdog expression tells a story all of its own.

"Drew."

"James. Up for a visitor?"

"Sure."

He leads me into his apartment. It's a mess. This was the kid who had the tidiest room out of all of us. Something's really wrong.

"What's going on?" I ask.

"Ashley left."

I sigh. That makes sense. James had a thing for Ashley long before they hooked up. It explains why he seems to have fallen off the rails. "I'm so sorry, mate. What happened?"

"She found someone else."

Shit. What the hell do I say to make this better? "I wish Hayley was here. She's so much better at this stuff than I am. But I'm telling you now, this isn't you, and you're worth more than this."

He blinks slowly. "Where's Hayley?"

"Heavily pregnant and tired. She's having a lie-in, and she's really sorry not to come."

James looks around the room. "Maybe it's just as well. She'd kill me for the way this place looks."

I chuckle. Since Hayley's been living in Hamilton with me, it's a much shorter trip to Auckland. We usually catch up with James when we visit, and they've gotten to know each other well. She's a bit of a mother hen when it comes to him. "She would. So sort your shit out so we can visit."

He straightens up. "I know I should, but—"

"Dude. This kind of thing is part of life. It sucks, but trust me, one relationship breakup can lead to something so much better. It did with Hayley and me, and when you're ready, it will for you. Clearly, Ashley wasn't the right one for you." I grip his shoulder. "Believe me. One day you'll look back on this, and it'll be a blip on your radar."

James nods. "I guess you're right."

"Bro, I'm always right."

He laughs. "You sound like Max."

"He's usually right too."

———

It's after one by the time I get back to Hayley's parents' place.

"Something smells good."

Sonya smiles. "Roast lamb for lunch. I know it's your favourite."

"Sounds amazing. How's Hayley been?"

"She's still upstairs. I've been in a couple of times to check on her, but she told me she was fine, just tired."

I nod. "Apparently carrying twins is exhausting."

"One baby was hard enough" She pats me on the arm. "Lunch will be ready in about twenty minutes."

"Thanks, Sonya."

I mount the stairs, two by two. As much as I loved seeing James, being with Hayley is more important to me right now. I've tried really hard to act like a husband and father-to-be than a doctor. She hates when I hover, and I understand that, but the reality is that multiple pregnancies are tough, and I want to make sure she doesn't want for anything.

"Hey." She's still in bed, right where I left her.

She gives me a lazy smile. "How was James? I thought you'd be back earlier."

"James is a mess. Ashley left him. I sat him down and told him to get his shit together."

"I'm so sorry to hear they broke up. I wish I'd seen him."

I smile. "Well, we're here for a couple more days. Maybe we can check in on him before we go."

"I'd like that."

Leaning over, I give her a tender kiss, waggling my eyebrows. "Your mum said lunch will be ready in about twenty minutes. How tired are you?"

She chuckles. "Never too tired for what I think you're suggesting."

Sex has been difficult the past few weeks with the added bulk of two babies. But it's not impossible.

I lie by her side and kiss her softly. She murmurs her approval, and I run my hand over her belly and lift her skirt, slipping into her panties and finding her clit with my fingers.

"You're already wet." There is a benefit to pregnancy hormones.

A husky laugh passes her lips. "I need you."

"I need you too." My hand slides farther down, and I pause. Something's not right.

"Babe, are you sure your waters haven't broken?"

"I think I might have noticed."

Sliding my hand out, my fingertips are coated in fresh blood.

Shit.

"Hayley? Are you just tired? Or are you having contractions too?"

She shakes her head. "No contractions. I'm not comfortable, but that's nothing new."

"I think I need to take a look at you."

"What's wrong?" Her words are a little slurred now, and she frowns.

Pulling her skirt and the blanket out of the way, I don't need to look much further. She's lying in a circle of her own blood, and it's so much more than I'd like to see.

I slide her panties down and examine her. It's not good.

Wiping my hand on the blanket to remove the blood, I take a look at her face. Her eyes are closed, and her skin's so pale. How did I not see it before?

"Hayley?"

Her eyelashes flutter as she opens her eyes, and she gives me a small, sad smile.

Grabbing my phone out of my pocket, I dial emergency services. "Ambulance, please."

The woman's talking at me, and I struggle to focus, but I have to. For Hayley.

"My name's Doctor Drew Campbell, and my wife has a suspected placental abruption. We need an ambulance as soon as possible."

I place the phone on speaker and put it on the bed. Hayley hiccups as a tear runs down her cheek. Of all the things for it to be, it had to be the thing that caused her patient's death five years ago. The thing that nearly ruined her career.

The irony isn't lost on me that she suffered so much for another woman's abruption, and here we are.

"Drew?"

"Back in a second, princess."

I open the door to find Sonya on the other side.

"Lunch is ready a little earlier than I thought," she says with a smile.

"Sorry, Sonya. Hayley's going to hospital. The ambulance is on its way."

"What?" Her eyes fill with worry.

I nod, holding my hand out to try and convey that I'm keeping calm for Hayley. Thankfully, she seems to pick up on it.

"What do you need me to do?"

"Just let them in when they get here. It'll be faster than me driving her, and they can monitor her the whole way."

"Is it serious?" she whispers.

I nod. The last thing I want is to frighten anyone. Hayley will be scared enough without anyone else panicking. But Sonya's strong. This woman once tried to set my girlfriend up with another guy right in front of me. She's got balls.

"I'll tell David and wait by the door."

Turning back to the bed, I lie beside Hayley and stroke her face. "Drew." Tears continue to fall, but she's remaining calm. At least on the outside.

"We'll get through this, princess. I promise."

She nods. "I trust you."

"I should have been here with you. You're so close, and I need to keep an eye on you."

"We didn't know."

I shake my head. "No, but I should be better at this. It's my job, and you're the most important person in the world to me."

Her smile's faint, but it still lights up the room. "And our babies."

I nod, but I know if it came down to it, I'd choose Hayley's life above all else. Even if it killed me.

"Those two have done fine, and they're old enough to be born now. Don't be scared."

It's easier said than done, but if anyone can handle this, it's Hayley. She knows the risks, but she also knows that these things can be mitigated by catching it early. I've seen worse than this and got the mother and baby through. There'd better be a good obstetrician waiting at the hospital.

There are three lives on the line.

HAYLEY'S PARENTS watch as she's carried to the ambulance on a stretcher. I jump in the back, and sit beside her.

"Hey," I say softly.

She gives me a small smile, but the strain in her expression is clear.

"How many patients do you think get their own personal obstetrician on the way to the hospital?"

Hayley laughs, and it's music to my ears.

One of the paramedics climbs in with me, and with sirens blaring we take off for the hospital.

This is about to be the longest ride of my life.

About halfway, I pull out my phone and dial. What I need is to hear the voice of the man who's my closest friend.

At the other end is Owen's cheery voice. "Hey. Am I an uncle again yet?"

"Not yet." I hold back, but my fear bubbles right at the surface. If this was a patient of mine, I'd know what to do. It's a whole different story trying to think clearly when it's the woman you love.

"Dude, what's wrong?"

"It's Hayley." Suddenly, this doesn't seem like such a good idea, and I'm not sure if I can get the words out. "She … she …"

"Slowly, mate. One word at a time." His tone's more serious now.

"We're on the way to the hospital. She has …" I can't complete the sentence.

"She has what?"

"Placental abruption."

There's silence for a moment. Owen knows Hayley's history. He and my other brothers were there for her when she needed them.

"Okay. I'm coming."

"You don't need to. I just wanted you to know."

"Let me call Ginny and deal with the kid. I'll hit the road as soon as I can."

"Thanks."

I hang up the call. There's no way I could say a lot more without breaking, and that's not what Hayley needs. She needs me to be strong because this road could be bumpy from here on in.

And she knows it.

25

OWEN

WHEN WE WERE GROWING UP, IT WAS ALWAYS COREY AND Adam, me and Drew. Spending twelve years of my life sharing a room with him, I developed a stronger bond with him than I did any of my other brothers.

"Are you okay to drive?" Ginny asks as she climbs into the car beside me.

"I'll be fine. You might just have to remind me to keep to the speed limit once in a while."

She shoots an annoyed glance at me and nods to the back seat. *Shit.*

"Looking forward to hanging out with Max for the night, Ava?"

Her little blonde head bobs up and down. I smile at her enthusiasm, and make a mental note to try not to imply we might crash. She still has dreams from time to time about that night.

"Max is so good with her. I bet they'll have heaps of fun,"

Ginny says, her light tone keeping the conversation upbeat. "You're doing the right thing, Owen. Drew needs you."

I'm acutely aware that I rely on Ginny so much where Ava's concerned. I don't know if I could do this without her. Reaching for her hand, I link her fingers with mine and drag her hand to the gearstick.

I called Adam as soon as I hung up from Drew. Their house is going to be Ava's sanctuary while yet more drama plays out in our lives. She doesn't need to know anything about it.

The thought of Hayley being in danger makes me sick.

Lily's on the steps when we pull in, concern written all over her face. I grab Ava's bag while Ginny helps her out of the car, and we walk toward my girl's auntie.

"Hi, Ava." Lily smiles, and I'm so grateful that she's happy to take Ava on top of dealing with Max and Rose. "Oh, and Owen and Ginny, of course."

"Ava." Max runs out, Lucky by his side. Ava giggles as the dog bowls her over and licks her cheek before Max pulls him off.

"Naughty," Max growls.

I hold out my hand to her. "You okay?"

She nods, wiping her face with the palm of her hand. "The doggy's tongue tickled."

"I bet it did." It's good to hear her laughter. She's so happy here.

"How's Hayley? Have you had any update?" Adam's right behind Max, his brows knitting in concern as he looks at me. We all know how much Drew loves Hayley, and if anything happened to her, it'd break him.

"No. I don't want to call Drew again. I'd imagine they'll

have all kinds of things going on. The sooner we get there, the sooner I'll let you guys know what's going on."

"What did he say when he called?" Lily asked.

"Something about placental abruption? I didn't have time to look it up, I just wanted to get Ava sorted so we could get out of here."

The colour drains from Lily's face.

"What is it? He was so stressed, I didn't want to stop and ask."

She swallows. "Hayley lost a patient in her second year to placental abruption. Though, in her case, she struggled to get a doctor to take it seriously in time."

"Drew's good. Can you imagine him? He would have been driving her crazy with his hovering." I lean over and kiss Lily on the cheek. Squatting, I smile at Ava. "Can you be a good girl for Adam and Lily?"

She nods, the happy expression disappearing from her face. I know she's pleased to be here, but that I'm leaving her is probably confusing. Even for the night.

"I need to go and check up on Auntie Hayley and the babies."

Her blue eyes widen. "The babies?"

I nod. "Remember? Two babies."

She throws her small arms around my neck, and I hold her tight. We've worked ourselves into this routine these past five months, and this is the first night we'll be apart. I thought this would be easy, letting her stay somewhere else, but my chest is tight at the thought.

I lift her off the ground, and nod at Adam. "Everything she needs is in her bag. There are pull-ups for night, and her pyjamas, a couple of changes of clothes, and a couple of toys."

She lets go of my neck, her big eyes still focused on me. "If you're a good girl for Uncle Adam, I'll have to see what I can bring home."

"Can I get a toy?"

"I'm sure we can find something." I plant a kiss on her nose and let her drop to the ground.

Max takes her by the hand. "Come on, Ava. I'm playing a racing game, but you can watch if you want."

As she disappears inside the house, I feel a twinge of regret I'm not taking her. But after what happened to her parents, the last place I think she needs to spend time in is the inside of a hospital.

"Thanks for everything," I say, not taking my eyes off the door she went through.

"It's never a problem. We can take her whenever you need a break." Lily smiles and slips her arms around my neck. "Give all our love to Drew and Hayley."

"I will." My voice breaks, and Ginny rubs my back.

It's time to get on the road.

26

DREW

I HOLD HER HAND TIGHT AS SHE'S WHEELED INTO THE HOSPITAL on a gurney. The ambulance crew radioed ahead, and there's a doctor waiting for us.

"Mrs Campbell, I'm Doctor Johnson." He smiles widely.

"Marcus?" Hayley's voice is strained and quiet.

I stare at the doctor who's arrived to take care of my wife.

"Hayley? I'm so sorry. I didn't recognise you at first."

"Doctor Marcus Johnson." He holds his hand out for me to shake. I ignore it.

"Is there anyone else who can help her. Quickly?" I ask.

"I'm it right now." He withdraws his hand.

"Shit."

"Drew, let him do it."

I fume. This is the man who nearly ruined Hayley's career. Do I want his hands on her? No.

Do I have much choice?

No.

"Look, Mr Campbell …" Marcus says.

"Doctor Campbell. Hayley's presenting with a class-two placental abruption, and there's far too much blood loss already. You'd better have your shit together."

He nods. "She's in safe hands, I promise."

Reluctantly, I take a step back. It sucks, but right now I don't have a choice. Hayley and the babies' fates are in this man's hands whether I like it or not.

"Well, Hayley, I'm glad you married a doctor, because at least I don't have to work out what I'm dealing with." He grabs the ultrasound wand and lifts Hayley's shirt. She takes a deep breath, and I walk around the other side of the bed so I can hold her hand and watch the monitor.

"Sorry, the gel will be cold."

"It's okay. I know."

He squirts gel on her belly, and runs the ultrasound wand across her baby bump. Our babies are active and healthy-looking, but I know what he's looking for because I'm looking too.

"How many weeks are you, Hayley?" he asks.

"Thirty-five."

He meets my gaze. "Good. I think these babies are going to make their appearance really soon."

I shift my focus back to the monitor, and he zooms in closer. The abruption is right there, and while it's not the worst I've ever seen, it's not good.

"We'll be good, Hayley. They'll be good. The most impor-tant thing is that the three of you are safe" I squeeze her hand.

She nods. "Whatever you two think."

Fear is in her eyes, and I lean over. "I'll be with you the whole way, princess."

"Of course you will."

"I'm not going to sugarcoat it because I think you both know exactly what's going on, but the best course of action is an emergency C-section. Your babies stand a good chance at this stage. Time is of the essence," Marcus says.

I nod. "I agree. But you'd better believe I'll be watching every move you make, and if you put a foot wrong ..."

He swallows.

"Drew, Marcus isn't a bad doctor."

My eyebrows raise at the sound of Hayley's words. Maybe she's right and he's a good doctor, albeit one who chose not to listen to her.

She gives me a wan smile. "I trust him. And I know you'll be there, watching over us."

"You'd better believe it."

While Hayley's being prepped for theatre, I scrub in with Marcus. I'll only be there watching, but I want to be as close to her as possible because I don't trust him.

"So, what area of medicine are you in?" he asks. "You picking up the abruption saved a lot of time."

"Obstetrics. Hayley and I live in Hamilton. We're just up here visiting her folks."

"And you landed here the weekend I'm on call."

"Well, then I guess this is it." I know my exasperation is clear in my voice, but I'd give anything for this to have happened at home where I know the hospital and the surgeons.

He nods. "I could call in another obstetrician, but the

other one on call lives out west, and I don't need to tell you that the sooner this is done, the better."

I suck in a breath. "Let me spell this out. If you put a foot wrong in that theatre, I'll find some way to ruin you."

He swallows hard and nods. "I understand."

"You owe her. Big time."

"She'll get the very best care."

"She'd better. If anything happens to her …"

The man I hate, but who will hold Hayley's life in his hands, grips my arm. "I've got her, Drew."

I can do nothing more than nod and trust that he can take care of everything.

It's weird being in an operating theatre and not being the one performing the operation.

Instead, I hold my wife's hand. This isn't going to be easy for her. She already needs transfusions to make up for the blood she's lost. Recovering from this is going to be long and tough, but Hayley's strong, and I'll be right by her side the whole way.

"I know this isn't what we planned, but it's the safest way." I stroke her cheek.

She squeezes my hand. "I know. As long as the babies are safe."

"As long as you're safe. You're my whole world, Hayley Campbell."

Hayley smiles. "I still love it when you call me that."

"You should be used to it by now. It'll be your name for

the rest of your life." I lean over and give her a tender kiss before straightening up and checking on Doctor Johnson.

"Ready, Hayley?" he asks.

"As I'll ever be," she replies.

As much as I hate this guy, I can't fault him in his work. He does everything by the book and as good a job as I'd do. It leaves me feeling grateful, and I hate that I feel that way about him.

"Baby number one." He lifts our first child out, and emotion overwhelms me.

"Drew?" Hayley's voice is so soft. This whole thing scares the shit out of her and rightfully so. It's easy in this situation for things to go pear-shaped and the mother and baby to be at risk.

I peer at our baby, and grin. "He's beautiful, Hayley. Small, but he looks perfect."

"He?"

I grin. For all the scans she's had, we haven't managed to catch what gender our babies are. Not that it's ever mattered. "We have a son."

She squeezes my hand, and I step back to let Marcus lay the baby on her chest. Hayley sighs contentedly.

"Here comes baby two," he says.

A little smaller, but no less perfect, appears my daughter. Tears well as I look at her in Marcus's hands. This is everything I've ever wanted—the wife I adore, and our children. *I'm a dad.*

For a moment, it punches me in the gut that Owen never got to have this moment. If Cara and Ryan hadn't died, he'd have been none the wiser about his child. And he missed seeing Ava come into the world.

Me? I'll never miss a thing when it comes to my kids. And I'm so grateful for that.

"You might need to help out here, Drew." Marcus lifts my daughter toward Hayley, laying the baby beside her brother.

Hayley's a blubbering mess, and I'm just as bad, sniffing as I press a kiss to her hand.

"They're here," she whispers.

"They're here, and they're safe."

With the babies covered in warm towels, we pay all our attention to them while Marcus works on completing Hayley's surgery and stitching her up.

My family's safe.

My family.

This moment has been coming for months, but it still seems surreal. For the rest of my life, I'll love Hayley and our children. I always wanted a big family, but after today, this is big enough.

I'm not putting Hayley through this again.

I know the odds are against this happening twice, but the thought of losing her leaves a hole in my chest so big you could drive a truck through it.

For years, I thought I wanted a big family, but if we never have more than these two, I'll be happy. I'm not sacrificing the love of my life for more babies.

The three people in front of me are everything.

They're all I need.

WE EXIT THE THEATRE, and time stands still as I watch my wife being wheeled in one direction, our babies in another.

Torn for a moment, I do the only thing I can and follow Hayley. The NICU here has a great reputation, and at this stage of gestation with the APGARs the babies got, I'm confident the children will be fine.

Hayley, on the other hand, still concerns me. By the time we left the theatre, she'd fallen asleep. Her faith in me is unwavering, but I had to swallow down my fear in there. He might have just saved her life, but Doctor Marcus Johnson is still a piece of shit as far as I'm concerned.

His hand lands on my back. "I've got her a private room as close to the NICU as I could. The next couple of days will be really tough as she recovers and is unable to get out of bed, but she's strong, and I'm sure you'll be at home with those babies really soon."

I turn to see his smile. "The sooner the better."

"I understand. She's just being taken to recovery, and once we're sure she's ready, she'll be moved to the ward."

"There's something else I need to discuss with you."

"What's that?"

He doesn't see my fist coming, and I slam him right in the face. Staggering, he hits the wall.

"You did a great job in there, but I've been dying to do that since I discovered what you did to her."

Holding his hand up with his other hand covering his cheek, he nods. "Drew, I—"

"You broke my girl, Johnson, and she is *so* strong and so good at her job. She'd have been a huge loss to the profession."

He nods. "I know. I'm sorry."

"It's not me who needs an apology. Just stay away from her."

Hayley's near the end of the corridor, and the bed turns left. I take off and follow, catching up just as the nurse turns it to take her into the room.

"You're not supposed to be in here," one of the nurses says.

"Tough."

She chuckles. "I'll go and get a chair. She's likely to sleep for a while. The whole experience can be exhausting."

I nod. "I've seen plenty of patients sleep after something so traumatic."

"You're a doctor?"

"An obstetrician."

A smile spreads across her face. "Then you won't get any argument from me about you being in here. How many patients get their own personal doctor in their room?"

She leaves to return a few moments later with a chair. It's not the most comfortable-looking thing, but I can deal with a little discomfort if Hayley's safe.

I pluck my phone out of my pocket. There's a text from Sonya.

Is there any news?

She's out of surgery and doing well. The babies are in the NICU, but they're both healthy. Congratulations, Grandma. It's a boy and a girl.

I can't help but smile as I type that last part. When I first met Sonya, I thought we'd never find common ground, but now she's as protective of me as she is of Hayley.

Stop with the grandma stuff. Let me know if you need anything and when we can visit.

Will do. I'll stay here for the night. They won't like it, but I'm not leaving.

Give our love to all our babies.

I look up at the ceiling with tears forming. Sonya's just at the end of the phone, but with Hayley unconscious, I feel so alone.

My phone buzzes again.

We're on our way.

Owen.

He said he'd come, but I wasn't sure if he would. He has commitments now—Ginny and Ava.

Thinking about them brings a smile to my lips. He always seemed so lost, but now, he's found with those two. He seems to be struggling a bit with fatherhood, but that'll come in time. Especially with Ginny's help.

I take a big breath, and Hayley stirs beside me. I'd give anything to hold her in my arms, to have our babies in this room too. But this is the deal we got, and of all people, I guess we should understand it.

Her eyes flicker open, and I smile at her as she fixes her tired gaze on me.

Leaning over, I stroke her temple. "You're in recovery, princess."

"The twins."

"They've gone straight to the NICU. They're so beautiful and healthy. I'm sure we'll all be together soon."

Her eyes fill with tears. "I want them with me. It's so unfair."

"Yeah, it is. And I'll do whatever I can to make that happen. Right now, I'm just really glad the three of you are safe. You scared the shit out of me."

"You stayed so calm."

I plant a gentle kiss on her forehead, lingering a few

seconds. "Only on the outside. I let your mother know, and I told her I'd spend the night with you."

She smiles. "I don't know if they'll let you."

"They can try and throw me out. I'm pretty sure Marcus still owes you a few favours."

Hayley licks her lips. "He probably saved my life."

"Maybe he did, but I figure it's the least he can do to make sure you have everything you need."

I lean over and give her another kiss. "Marcus said when you were ready, they'd move you to a room near the NICU. When you're able to get out of bed, it won't be far to see the twins."

"I need them, Drew."

"I know you do. And I'll do whatever I can to make that happen as soon as I can."

She nods. "I know you will."

"The twins are in good hands. It's you I'll be hovering over. You lost a lot of blood, and you know I worry anyway."

Hayley reaches for my hand. "I know you do. We'll all be okay because you got us here."

"I wish I'd got you here sooner."

Her eyelids droop, and I can see just how much this has taken out of her.

"Get some sleep, princess. I'll be right here when you wake up."

Her breathing slows. I don't have to tell her twice.

27

OWEN

WE GET HALFWAY THERE BEFORE GINNY KICKS ME OUT OF THE driver's seat.

"I'll keep us at the speed limit," she says.

She's my calm when all I want to do is storm.

Right now, I'm angry at the world for what's happening to Drew and Hayley. I'd do anything to make Hayley better.

I stare out the window at the paddocks we pass on the open road. The sooner we get there, the better.

"I hope Hayley's okay." Ginny's so soft-spoken, but she wakes me out of my trance, and I turn to look at her.

"So do I. They don't deserve this. I mean, no one does, but not those two."

"Has Drew sent you any more texts?"

I sigh. "No, and he didn't reply to the last one I sent him. But if she's in surgery, I'm sure they're just busy." My grip on my jeans tightens, thinking of the alternative.

"At least she's married to an obstetrician, so he'll have got her the care she needs. He'll know what to do."

Losing her would kill him.

Glancing at Ginny, my chest tightens. *Just like losing you would kill me.*

"I love you, Ginny."

She shoots a glance at me, and gives me a small smile. "I love you too."

"I know it's not the first time I've said it, but I need you to know in case anything ever happens to me." I close my eyes. "Shit. What would I do with Ava if something happened to me?"

"That's all part of you becoming a dad, Owen. You need a plan. She's lost everything once, so you need to make sure that she's got a safe, secure home no matter what."

I nod. "When we get back, I'll talk to Adam and Lily. They're the most obvious choice."

"They'd be a good option. It's never nice to think about the what ifs, but when there are kids involved …"

Letting out a loud breath, I smile. "Ava's been with me for five months, and I'm so disorganised still. I should have thought about this early on. I've got a will—had to get it done when I bought the bakery. Drew gets it all in the event of my death, we planned it together ages ago, but it'll have to change."

Ginny reaches for my hand and squeezes.

"Of course, if you move in with us, it'll all change again."

"Owen." Her tone is pained.

"We need you, Gin. Ava loves you, and so do I. I know things haven't gone the way we thought they would, but we've got through the disruption of the past few months and we're so strong."

She nods. "I know. Can we talk about it later? We're not far from Auckland."

"Sure."

I don't know if she genuinely wants to talk about it later, or if the answer's still just no and she doesn't want to let me down right now.

Ginny has to be ready.

Ava and I both need her.

THE HOSPITAL IS a maze of corridors, and it takes a while to find where we're supposed to be.

I round a corner and stop on the spot when I see Drew. He's sitting in a row of chairs in the wide corridor, his shoulders slumped and his head down. My heart stops.

"Drew?"

He raises his head, and I can see the exhaustion in his face. Behind me, Ginny grips my shoulder.

Something's wrong. He's not the happy, smiley man he usually is.

He gives me a tired smile. "Hey."

"I got here as fast as I could. Thought you could do with some support. Corey's gone bush, and Adam and Lily have got Ava."

He nods. "I'm glad you're here."

"What's going on?"

His smile widens. "We've got a boy and a girl. They're

small and in the NICU, but the birth was much more traumatic than it should have been. Hayley lost a lot of blood."

"Where is she?"

He nods at the door opposite. "In there. She's sleeping at the moment. I just needed a minute."

"So they're all okay?"

Nodding again, he stands as I walk toward him. As we embrace, he's trembling. "I thought I was going to lose her. Or them. All those years of training and I couldn't even help my own wife."

"Dude, some things are always going to be out of your control. Now, can I see the babies?"

He chuckles and lets go of me, taking Ginny's hand and leaning over to kiss her on the cheek. "Of course you can. I'll just pop my head in and check on Hayley."

Stepping across the corridor, he opens the room and leans in. "Hey. You up for some visitors?" A second later, he turns back to us. "Come in."

Hayley's pale, but her smile still lights up the room. "Owen, Ginny, it's so good to see you."

I wink. "Couldn't stay away."

"Have you seen my babies?"

I shake my head, and sit on the bed, taking her hand in mine. "Not yet, but Drew's taking us to them."

She swallows hard as she squeezes my hand. "I'm not allowed out of bed yet. Give them a cuddle from me."

"That sucks."

"It does, but we're all safe. Thanks to Drew."

I turn my head, but he's across the room by the window. I wasn't imagining things. There's something up with him.

"Drew?" Hayley's voice wobbles. Drew's not even making eye contact with her, and it scares me.

He shakes his head. "It's my fault you were in danger to start with."

"What are you talking about?" she asks.

"I should have been better. I should have picked up on the signs earlier. Now, you're stuck here and you can't even touch our babies. You should be angry with me."

Bewilderment fills her expression. "You got us all here in one piece, and you knew what was going on. If it hadn't been for you, it could have easily been worse. You saved our lives." Her chest rises and falls as she appears to hold back a sob.

Ginny steps closer and rubs Hayley's arm as if attempting to comfort her. "Drew, get your arse over here and look after your woman before she gets upset and this equipment starts beeping or something."

I push myself off the bed and turn to face him. His face tells the story of a man struggling with his emotions. A couple more heavy breaths, and he crosses the room. Hayley reaches for him, cupping his face.

"Can you forgive me for not picking up what was going on sooner?"

Tears roll down her cheeks. "There's nothing to forgive."

I look away when they kiss, and Ginny slips her arm around my waist. Closing my eyes, I lean my head on top of hers.

"We made two beautiful babies," Hayley whispers.

"Maybe we'll hold back from breeding that rugby team." Drew's response makes me smile.

I give them a moment, waiting until Drew pulls back from Hayley.

"How about you take me to meet my niece and nephew? Then we can come back here and spend some more time with Hayley."

Hayley nods. "That's a wonderful idea." Her eyes are still a little hazy, and she has a wistful look on her face. I feel a bit shit for even suggesting it.

"If you're okay for a bit, I'll pop to the NICU. Be back really soon." Drew gives her another kiss. "Love you."

"Love you too."

It's with a heavy heart that I leave Hayley alone in the room. I can't even imagine what Drew feels like. As we make our way down the corridor, Ginny grabs my hand.

I meet her gaze. Her expression tells me she feels the same way I do. God, how I love this woman. I want with her what Drew has with Hayley—marriage, children, the lot.

What used to terrify me is now a dream.

It's not far to the NICU. Hayley's close to her children, and once she's mobile, she'll be able to see them in minutes.

Drew beams as he leads us toward two incubators in the corner of the room. "Here they are."

I gasp when I see them, and Ginny has a similar reaction. They're early and small, but Drew's children are perfect. I only know which is which from the little signs on the incubators that say 'Baby girl Campbell' and 'Baby boy Campbell'. They're both alive and alert. All they need is their mother.

"Owen?" Ginny grips my arm.

"Yes?"

She sweeps her hand across my face. "You've got tears in your eyes. I know why. They're beautiful."

"I want this," I say without thinking.

Ginny licks her lips, and nods.

"I never thought I'd want anything like this, but I want it all with you." I turn to her, my heart seizing at the sad look on her face. *Shit.*

It's her turn to tear up. "We need to talk about it."

"We'll do all the talking when we get home." I grasp her elbow, and place a gentle kiss on her cheek.

Drew stands between the incubators, a hand resting on each one. Love's written all over his face, and the three of us struggle with tears. Drew's eyes are only for his children.

"I hate that Hayley can't come and see them. And I can't take them to see her."

"There's one thing we can do if she's got her phone," I say.

He frowns. "Call her?"

"No, you dummy. She's got an iPhone too, right? We can FaceTime her."

His face lights up, as if I've given him a gift. "Why didn't I think of that?"

"Because you might have the medical degree, but I got the brains of the family."

He nudges my arm and rolls his eyes, pulling his phone out of his pocket. "Babe," he says as it makes contact.

"What are you doing?" she asks.

"Take a look for yourself."

He turns his phone toward the incubators, and a gasp comes from Hayley on the other end. "I can't bring you to our babies, but I can kind of bring them to you."

She's crying, I can hear it, but they're tears of happiness. It leaves me itching to get home and pick up Ava. I won't see my little girl until tomorrow.

My heart aches. Until now, Ava has been the daughter I never knew, the one who had two parents and was only with me because of tragic circumstances. But she is my little girl, and I've missed all her milestones. I've missed everything.

I wasn't there to see her crawl, or walk, or hear her talk for the first time. I missed every day of her growing up until now, and when I go home, I don't intend to miss another thing.

"Here's our little girl. I don't know about you, but I think she deserves a name." Drew laughs. "So does our son."

"We'll work that out. Can you take some photos and send them to me?" Hayley asks.

I pull my phone out and send a quick text to Adam.

Can you take a photo of Ava and send it to me?

Ginny squeeze my arm. "I hope Hayley's reunited with them soon."

I smile. "So do I."

Sure. She's asleep though.

I just realised I don't have any photos of my daughter.

My heart is in my throat. She's *my* daughter. From now on, Ava will feel loved and wanted. She'll be my spoiled little princess.

I suck in a breath as the image arrives.

My little angel. She's fast asleep with her thumb firmly in her mouth. I love her, and for the first time I really feel like I'm her father. Only it sucks, because I'm so far away and I can't hug her and tell her. It's been such a confusing time for her, and I don't think I've been there the way I should have. I've been on autopilot, working to a routine as she settled, but not taking the time to make that final emotional step.

"She's beautiful," Drew says, looking over my shoulder.

"I'm her dad," I say, as if it's the first time I've ever told him.

Ginny reaches for my chin and drags my gaze to hers. Those green eyes search my own. "Owen, are you okay?"

"I'm a dad, Ginny."

She smiles and wipes away the tears I didn't even know were there. "Yes, yes you are."

"Why didn't you tell me I was being a dick?"

She laughs softly. "Because you weren't. And because Ava is fine, and you needed time to work it all out in your head."

"Ava needs me."

"She does, Owen. She needs all of us. Well, all of you. That little girl needs her family."

I wrap an arm around her waist and pull her closer. "You're part of that family."

"Can you two have a moment outside of the NICU?" Drew laughs. "I want to get back to Hayley. I'm thinking about now she's looking at the photos I just took and she needs me." He stands between the incubators and places a hand on each one. "I'll be back in a little bit with some food." Shaking his head at us, he laughs. "Hayley's about to feel like a dairy cow."

"You call your wife a cow and I'm pretty sure she'll rip your head off."

He kicks at my ankle. "That's not what I'm saying, and you know it."

I smile, because nothing can faze me now. I've got my girls, and my niece and nephew will be fine. It won't be long before Hayley can see them, and Drew has everything he's ever wanted.

And I do too.

28

OWEN

The sound of Ava giggling hits me before I see her. After everything, it's an amazing sound to hear, and Ginny grips my shoulder and smiles.

"Do you know what?" she asks.

"What?"

"When her parents were still here, it was just the three of them. You've opened her world, Owen. She has aunties and uncles and cousins."

I nod. "You're right. I'll always make sure she remembers her parents, but I'll also make sure she has lots of good new memories.

"I'll see you inside." She pecks me on the cheek, and walks up the steps to the door of Adam and Lily's house.

My daughter's close.

I know for sure she's become part of the family as she comes around the corner of the house perched on Corey's shoulders. He's the tallest of all of us, and she shrieks with laughter, wobbling as she points at me.

"Should we go see him?" Corey asks.

"Yes." She's all high-pitched squeals as he pretends she'll fall. I know he'll never let that happen, but I widen my eyes and open my mouth to show fear.

"Isn't that dangerous?" I ask.

She shakes her head. "Corey made me taller than Max."

"Sweetheart, you're taller than everyone. You might disappear up into the clouds."

She leans over and reaches for me. Corey stoops so I can pull her off his shoulders and into my arms.

I hug her tight, burying my face in her neck, and she giggles as I plant kisses on her jaw.

"That tickles."

"Have you been a good girl?"

Ava nods.

"We've been playing in the bush out the back. We found some wetas," Corey says.

I screw up my face. "Ewww."

She gapes. "They were all icky. But Corey's not scared of them."

He shrugs. "They're just bugs."

"Did you bring me a present?" she asks.

"Let me think. Maybe." I grin.

"Owen," she growls, and Corey and I both laugh.

"Come on." I carry her to the car, and open the back door. On the back seat is a huge shopping bag, and her eyes widen.

"Is that for me?"

"No, it's for Lucky. It's a giant dog bone."

She laughs. "No, it's for me."

"Better grab it then."

Tugging at the handles of the bag, she pulls it out the door and onto the ground. "I need help," she says.

"Thought you might. How about we go inside so I can see Adam and Lily, and you can take a look at what's in the bag?"

She nods, and we turn back toward the house. I pick up the bag, and she skips ahead of me and in the front door.

"Hey, how's Hayley doing?" Corey asks.

"She'll be okay. They've got a lot to work through. She lost a heap of blood during the birth, and she's stuck in the ward while the babies are in the NICU, so it's upsetting for her. Drew's going to be going back and forward a bit between them. But she and the babies will be fine, and they'll all be home by next week if things continue to go well."

He nods. "That's a relief. Drew worships her. After everything they had to deal with getting together, you'd think this bit would be easy."

"Nothing's ever easy. I mean, I just became a dad to a four-year-old. How weird is that?"

Ava stands in the doorway, her arms crossed, and frowns. "Owen. Hurry up."

"Yeah, hurry up, *Owen*." Corey laughs.

I roll my eyes and head toward the door.

Inside, Lily and Ginny sit in the corner, talking quietly. Max is on the console in front the TV, and Adam's with him.

"Hey," Adam says. "Ginny was just catching us up about Drew and Hayley. You okay?"

I nod. "Yeah, Drew was a bit of a mess, but they're getting there."

He shifts his gaze to Ava. "You've got a very talkative daughter. Once she started, she wouldn't stop."

I laugh. "It's good for her."

Ava tugs on my arm. "Bag?"

I place it on the ground, and she pulls out a soft toy rabbit, a My Little Pony toy, and a box of Lego.

"I didn't know what you wanted, so I got you a few things."

Ava holds the rabbit in her arms, snuggling it tight. "I love this." She looks up. "Thank you."

"You're welcome, sweetheart."

She stands, wrapping her arms around my legs to hug me. I struggle to hold in tears. She's as attached to me as I've become to her.

Ava is going to be just fine.

And she's all mine.

Ava's saying her final goodbyes, and I pack the car with her things.

Even though she's only been living with me these past few months, it feels wonderful to be taking her home. *Our* home.

There's only one thing missing from it.

Ginny appears in the doorway, and makes her way down the steps toward the car. "She's saying goodbye to Lucky. I think he's licking her to death."

I laugh. "She'll have to come here more often. It's good for her."

"You could always just get a dog."

I shrug. "I always steered clear of pets. Not really good if they get into the kitchen. Health regulations and all."

"True."

"All I want to do is get some sleep. Tomorrow, I'll look at extending Tammy's hours. Mel's wanted some more responsibility. Maybe it's time to give it to her."

Ginny nods. "She'll be done with her apprenticeship soon. It might be a good way to keep her."

"That too." I slide my arms around her waist. "What I want is to be able to sleep in with you sometimes when you stay the night. Can't be fun when I disappear at four in the morning."

She shrugs. "I knew what I was getting into with you. At least, in that regard."

"What didn't you know?"

"That I would fall crazy in love with a man who never stayed still. But who stayed still for me."

I hug her, planting a kiss on her neck. "You're worth staying still for."

"Are we going home now?" Ava says, walking down the steps.

"Yes, we are, sweetheart."

She beams.

"We'll finally get working on painting that room this week. What colour did you want?"

"Purple," she shrieks.

I laugh. "Steady on. It's not *that* exciting."

"Ava, I think we might need to go for a drive and find you a new duvet cover to match your room. Let's make it really pretty," Ginny says.

Ava draws level with Ginny and grabs her hand. I love how it's just second nature for her to do that. She loves Ginny as much as I do.

"Let's get you in the car." Ginny walks with Ava, pulling open the back door. She buckles her into the car seat before standing and smiling. "We're ready."

I tug open the passenger door, and she climbs in, patting me on the chest as she does. More than anything, I love the idea of going home with both Ginny and Ava.

As I pull out of Adam's driveway, and turn into the street. Ginny places her hand on my knee. "I think we need to stop at my place on the way."

My heart sinks. It's been good to be home, but I had hoped Ginny would stay with us tonight. We're at the point where maybe we can feel like a family, and I need her with me. "You can stay with us."

She grins. "I am. I just want to grab some more things. Hope that invite to move in is still open."

"Really?"

Ginny reaches for my hand. "There are still things we need to talk about. But all I wanted was for you to work out the whole dad thing. I think you've got that sorted."

"What do you think, Ava? Should we let Ginny move in?"

"Yes," Ava screeches, and I chuckle as I turn right instead of left and head toward Ginny's place.

We *are* a family.

DESPITE MY EXHAUSTION, I'm up at four as usual. The drive to and from Auckland wore me out, and sleeping in a strange bed even for a single night left my back aching.

Funny how I used to do that often and not notice it.

I get through most of the baking, but after about the fiftieth yawn, Mel growls.

"Go back to bed for a bit. I'll open up. You need all the time you can get with your family." Mel pushes me toward the flat.

I sigh. "Well, if you insist."

"Tammy will be here soon. We've got this."

"You're the best." I open the door.

"I know I am."

Grinning as I leave the kitchen and enter the flat, I know the bakery's in safe hands.

Ginny's still fast asleep, and snuggled in tight beside her is Ava. Neither of them stir as I enter the room.

Slipping into bed, I press a kiss on the back of Ginny's head.

"Hrmm?" She chuckles. "How long has Ava been here?"

"I was going to ask you that."

"Just as well I put your shirt on after you left. I got cold."

I reach over her and stroke Ava's hair. "I'm glad she feels safe enough to climb into bed with you."

"Me too. She's doing really well. You two are good for each other," she whispers.

Ginny rolls onto her back, and I gaze at her in the dim light. From the small gap in the curtains, the streetlight outside illuminates the room enough that I can see her eyes, so full of feeling.

"You're good for me. More than you even realise."

A smile spreads across her face, and she lifts a hand to stroke my cheek. "I love you, Owen Campbell."

"I love you too. How about I move the munchkin and I show you just how much?"

She nods. "Sounds good to me."

Sliding back out of bed, I cradle Ava in my arms. She stirs, but rests her head against my chest. For a moment, I take her in. My heart's never been so full.

All those years ago, I made a decision that left me drifting and alone. Now, I look back and realise just how empty my life was until I had Ginny and Ava. I'm the luckiest son-of-a-bitch alive to fall in love twice in a matter of months, and to have both ladies in my life. I never want to lose this feeling.

"Owen?" Ginny murmurs.

"Just making sure she's asleep. Don't want her to wake up and be back in here in five minutes' time."

"Good thinking."

I carry Ava to her bed and lower her gently into it. Pulling over the blanket, I bend and plant a soft kiss on her forehead.

Ginny's waiting when I return, her arms open and a smile on her face. "Is she okay?"

"Still asleep. God, Gin, I just love you both so much." I slide in beside her, and roll into her embrace.

"You were going to show me something?" She waggles her eyebrows. Her breath quickens as I slide my hand up her shirt and pinch her nipple before dropping it between her legs.

"Hrmm," I murmur into her neck as my fingers do their quick work. "Come here."

I flip onto my back and pull her with me, reaching for the box of condoms. Those long legs of hers straddle me, and when the condom's on, she pushes herself up, sliding back down onto my cock. She's in control.

Her milky skin glows as the sun peeps in the window. I

could start my day every morning like this from now on. Maybe I will.

She shivers, and I run my hands up her arms to her shoulders, pulling her down to kiss her. I thrust my hips up to meet the rocking of hers, and all I know is that this is meant to be. It always was.

"Owen," she whispers. Her breasts rub against my chest, and we're almost parallel. Stroking her back, I run my hands down to grip her arse, pulling her against me. The perfect angle.

"That's it, baby," I murmur.

"Owen, I …" She doesn't finish her sentence as her eyes widen. The sight of Ginny coming is a beautiful thing, and never more so than when I'm inside her.

"Love me?" I tease.

She laughs, and it sends ripples through my body, leaving me moaning.

"Always."

I bite at her bottom lip as I come. This really is the way I want to start each and every day from now on

I've never been happier.

WE SLEEP for a while before the alarm goes off at seven.

Ginny stirs beside me.

"We should think about getting out of bed. Ava's got day care, and you've got work," I say.

"Can't we just stay in bed?" She snuggles in.

"Not for long. We might have got Miss Ava back to her own bed, but she'll be up soon."

She smiles. "We'll never be able to sleep in, will we?"

Laughing, I plant a kiss on her neck. "One day, when she's older. Although maybe one day we'll grow our family and still have to deal with being up all hours of the night." I grin. "Then there are my four o'clock starts."

I expect a laugh, but Ginny's silent.

"Gin?"

"There's something I need to tell you." Her voice is barely louder than a whisper. But I have an inkling of what's coming.

"What?"

Ginny rolls onto her back, and cups my cheek in her hand. "I don't know if I can have children." Tears well in her eyes, and I lean in, kissing each one as she closes her eyes.

"Talk to me."

"I have endometriosis. It could make it really difficult." She sighs.

I search her eyes and see only sadness. It stings my heart to see her like this. "It's not the end of the world for me, Ginny. Whatever happens, as long as I have you, that's all that matters. Look at how Ava came to us. We could always foster or adopt if it doesn't work out."

She blinks back more tears. "Are you sure? I know we should have talked about this before I moved in. But it caused so many problems in my last relationship. He didn't understand. And then it never seemed like the right time, and—"

I cut off her sentence with a lingering kiss. "I'm sure. I never thought I'd be so lucky as to have someone like you in my life. Besides, we have Ava to raise, and that little girl is going to be spoiled beyond belief if you're not here to rein me in."

Ginny laughs, and the smile lights up her eyes. "Yes, we do have Ava to raise."

"We're all together, and that's everything."

"One of the reasons I wasn't sure about moving in is that sometimes I struggle with pain. I didn't want Ava to see that."

I nod. "We'll work through it with her together. I'm assuming that's why you're on the diet?"

"The doctor suggested it might help. There are studies …"

"Does it help?"

She shrugs. "It's hard to know what helps. I'll try anything."

"We can talk to Drew."

Her eyebrows dip. "I don't know if I want to talk to your brother about my uterus."

"I meant, he can refer us to someone. As if I'd let him anywhere near you. He must have a woman doctor he can suggest."

Her concerned expression gives way to laughter, and I grin, as that's what I wanted to see.

"You're not alone now, Ginny. That's the important thing. And you can tell me anything. I'll be right here beside you." I kiss her again, and lose myself in her until I hear little footsteps approaching.

"Owen." Ginny giggles.

"I heard."

The door flies open. "Breakfast," Ava yells.

I laugh. "Ava. Aren't you supposed to knock?"

Her eyes widen. "Sorry."

"Come here."

She climbs onto the bed, and I pull her into my arms for a hug. "I think someone wants breakfast."

"Really?" Ginny says. "Whatever gives you that idea?"

"Just a hunch."

Ava wraps her arms around my neck, and I hold her tight.

Whether or not Ginny and I have a baby of our own one day doesn't matter.

I have everything I need right here.

29

DREW

I spend the night at the hospital.

By the morning, the colour's returned to Hayley's cheeks. The blood transfusions have worked a treat for her, and all she has to really worry about now is resting to recover from her C-section.

We just have to wait for the all-clear so I can grab a wheelchair and take her to the NICU.

As soon as the ward opens, Sonya appears in the doorway with a bouquet of flowers and two congratulatory balloons, one blue, one pink.

"Mum." Hayley tears up again. She's shed tears on a fairly regular basis since the babies were born yesterday. It makes sense. Her hormones will be raging, plus the added stress of surgery and being separated from the twins. There's nothing I can do to help but be there for her.

Sonya enters the room, followed by David. While the two

women hug and chat, he comes toward me, hand extended. "Congratulations, Dad."

I grin. "Thanks, Grandad."

He grips my arm. "You did well, Drew. That they all got through it is testament to the man and doctor you are. I keep thinking if we'd only checked on her more thoroughly earlier …"

"I'm not sure when the bleeding started. And it's perfectly reasonable to be tired that late in a pregnancy. Especially a multiple pregnancy. You had no reason to think otherwise."

He nods. "I know. I just wish we'd been able to do something to reduce the trauma."

"Once she's reunited with the twins, she'll be so much better."

"How are they?"

I pull out my phone. I sent them some photos by text yesterday, but there is a whole heap more on there now. I've been the one travelling back and forward to feed them. Hayley's persisted with using the breast pump even though she's been exhausted.

"They're young enough that they might not have the reflex to breastfeed, so they're tube-fed right now. It's the best way to feed them directly, and it gives them a better chance of learning to breastfeed. We don't want them getting used to a bottle unless we have to."

He nods. "Hayley was a little early, but nothing like this. They're getting the best of care?"

"They are." I huff. "Though you might not like who her doctor is."

"Who?"

"Marcus Johnson."

I don't need to explain any more as his jaw drops. "You're kidding. Was there no one else?"

Shaking my head, I sigh. "I made it clear if he put a foot wrong I'd ruin his career."

The corners of David's mouth curl, and he gives me a proud look.

"And then I hit him."

"You did what?"

"After the surgery. Once I knew Hayley was safe. I smacked him in the face. It's probably a miracle I didn't get thrown out of the hospital."

David laughs. "I would have sorted that out. It's nothing that man doesn't deserve."

"I couldn't help it. I watched him perform the C-section, deliver our children, stitch Hayley back up, but it wasn't enough. He caused so much damage to her."

He grips my shoulder. "She's so much stronger now. I'm so proud of both of you." Letting go of my shoulder, he nods toward Sonya. "We've decided we'll wait to see the babies. It's not fair if we spend time with them when Hayley hasn't been able to."

"My brother arrived yesterday, and we went to the NICU. He spent more time worrying about his daughter back home and not a lot looking at the babies, but he did come up with the idea to FaceTime Hayley from the NICU. It works a treat."

David grins. "How is Adam?"

"Oh, not that brother. Owen."

His eyebrows knit. "I thought only Adam had children."

"It's a long story. Short version is that after the wedding, Owen ended up with a daughter he didn't know he'd fathered. She's living with him now, and I'm so glad because that poor kid got shipped around after her mother died. It's reinforced the fact that I'll have everything sorted so that Hayley and the kids are provided for after I'm gone."

He nods. "I'm going to make sure you're all well looked after, too. And it sounds like Owen's daughter's in a better place now."

"Very much so."

"And now you have two of your own to raise." He smiles. "I'll be retiring later in the year. It's time. There's nothing I want more than to be able to spend time with my grandchildren."

"I'm sure Hayley will love that, too. We might have to stay at your place for a couple of days before we head home. I don't want to rush her."

"When will she be able to go home?"

"Maybe in a week or so. The babies are doing well, but we need to get their feeding established, or at least on the way to that, and they need to gain weight. But I think they're a little bit further along than we thought, just small, so that might not be too tough a battle."

He nods. "Anything you two need. Between you and me, Sonya is more than ready to go out and buy two of everything for our place so you can stay whenever you need to."

"I can buy portable cots. At least the car seats are sorted and in the car, so I don't have to go and do that."

David claps me on the back. "Leave it with us. We'll sort everything out."

It's hard to say yes to. The one thing I've been looking forward to doing is being able to support my family without help. But I know under current circumstances, it's easier to swallow my pride and let him and Sonya take care of things.

Then I can focus on Hayley and the babies.

IT'S NEARLY midday when Marcus appears.

"Sorry I'm late. Another emergency. But I'm pleased to tell you that from what I've been told, you'll be able to get out of bed and see your children today. I know it must have been hard."

Hayley's all tears again, and I slip my arm around her shoulder.

He turns to me. "There's a wheelchair being brought in. Hayley can go to the NICU to see the babies. Just don't let her do any lifting."

I grin. "I'll make sure I hand her the twins."

"I know you'll take the best care of her." He turns to walk away, looking over his shoulder as he reaches the door. "For what it's worth, Hayley, I should have listened to you. You're an excellent midwife." He nods toward me. "And I reckon you've found a good one here."

She reaches for my hand as he disappears. "I never thought that would happen."

"Maybe I punched some sense into him."

Her mouth falls open. "You did what?"

"I couldn't help it. He understood. It wasn't the most adult thing I've ever done, but it felt so good."

A smile spreads across her face. "I love you."

"I love you. And I'll always do whatever it takes to protect you and the kids."

"I know."

Five minutes later, a wheelchair is brought in and I help Hayley into it. She's in tears before we make it all the way into the room. She moves to stand, and I place a hand on her shoulder, pushing her gently back into the chair.

"I'll get them."

I go to our daughter first. The nurse smiles as I open the incubator and take her out. The twins are developed enough that they can come out for us to hold. They just need help keeping warm to stabilise their blood sugar. "Here she is."

Hayley gasps, and I place one baby in her arms. Tears roll down her cheeks as she holds our daughter close, and my eyes prick with my own tears watching them.

"Do you want a minute with her before I get the other one?"

She nods. I think if I place both twins in her arms, she'll melt down.

"I've missed you," she whispers, raising the baby to place a gentle kiss on her forehead.

"She's missed her mum. But she's doing so well. They both are. It won't be long before we can all go home together."

Hayley nods, reaching for me with her free hand. "I'm sorry if I'm crying a lot right now."

"You have nothing to be sorry for, princess. The last few days have been a rollercoaster."

"She's so beautiful, Drew. We made her."

"We did good."

She lets go of my hand and strokes the baby's cheek. "She's my princess."

I lean over, pressing a kiss in her hair. "Yes, she is. Want me to get our little prince?"

"Yes, please." Her eyes shine, and I love how happy she looks. After a very stressful couple of days, Hayley has all she needs right here.

Going to the incubator, I take our son out. Hayley holds her arm to take him, and for a moment, she's holding both our children. It's the most beautiful thing I think I've ever seen. "I'll take her in a second, but I want a photo."

Tears stream down her face again, and she laughs. "Don't you dare show anyone what a mess I am."

"You're allowed to be. And no one needs to see this. It's for me." I snap the picture with my phone. "The three loves of my life all together."

"Drew," she says softly.

"Love you all." I reach for my daughter while she studies our son. My heart swells at the sight of this tiny creature with her perfect fingers and toes, her big blue eyes. She's just as beautiful as her mother, and she owned me at first glance.

They all do.

My family.

CHAPTER 30

OWEN

We spend the next few days moving Ginny's stuff into my place.

My flat is full, but so is my heart. The three of us are finally a family. Although it's been like that for months, having Ginny with us all the time makes it more real.

We go to bed the first night, and I look around the room. A few days ago, it was all my clothing, and a few items of Ginny's. Now there are boxes stacked in the corner, her things overflowing from them. But now I have my girl here, a little mess doesn't matter.

"I love this," she says, climbing into the bed beside me.

I pull her into my arms. "This is just the start."

"What do you mean?"

I kiss her, long and slow, stroking her breast. "We're right at the beginning. There's so much more good stuff for us to come. I'm sure of it."

She scans my face. "I love you. I love Ava. I love being with both of you."

"This is where you belong."

Ginny lets out a contented sigh as I drop my head to her breast, suckling at her nipple where my hand's been. She's mine, but I feel the need to claim her all over again. This really is the first night of the rest of our lives. Together.

Running my fingers down between her breasts and over her stomach, I keep my attention on her nipple as I find her clit with my fingers. I stroke her gently, and the tiny gasps coming from her lips tell me she likes it.

"I want you inside me," she whispers, thrusting her hips toward me.

"All in good time. There's no rush."

Her body tenses, and I bite down gently on her nipple. I want every little piece of her tonight, and I want her to feel everything. She needs to know just how much she's loved and wanted.

She shudders, letting out a long, low moan. I love this woman. I love that she's the only one I've had in my bed, and that she'll be the only one.

Her fingers rake my scalp when I go down on her. I'm so in tune with her body, I know how far I can take her, how much I can push. She's perfect, and she's mine.

"Roll over."

She stares at me for a moment, fear in her eyes. The last time we tried this, she said I was in too deep and hurt her. Now I know what the problem is, maybe we can work with what we can do. "Owen?"

"Do you trust me?" I grab a condom from the drawer.

She nods, and rolls onto her stomach.

"Get up on your knees and lean back."

I pull her into almost a sitting position. From here, she can control how deep I go, and I get to touch her.

Sliding her onto my cock, I move slowly, my hands on her hips to show her just how in control she is. Reaching up, I grasp her breasts, planting kisses on her back as she drives us together.

"All I want is for you to feel safe with me. To know I won't hurt you," I whisper.

"I've always felt safe with you."

We move so slowly, but I wouldn't have it any other way. One day she'll trust me, and we'll ditch the condoms. I haven't even approached that conversation yet, but the thought of being inside her without them drives me crazy.

"Owen." She throws her head back, and I slip one hand down to her clit, stroking and teasing until her pussy grips me tighter.

I'm almost caught by surprise by my own climax, triggered by hers, and we fall onto the bed in a sweaty, happy mess.

"I just need to get rid of this." I pull the condom off, and push myself up.

She grabs my arm. "I'm on the pill. It helps with the endo."

I grin. It's so tempting, but there's something I need to get done first. Something I want to do for her.

"I'll get tested first. I usually get tested for my annual check-up, but I should have done it when we first got together."

Ginny nods, a smile spreading across her lips.

I'll do whatever it takes to make Ginny happy.

When I climb back into bed, she curls up beside me, my arm under her neck. It doesn't take long for her breathing to even out, and I know she's fallen asleep.

"I love you," I whisper into her hair.

Because I do. From the day I looked into those green eyes for the first time, I was smitten. Even if back then, I didn't realise just how much. Her caring nature, her complete acceptance for my changing situation, her calmness—everything about Ginny leaves me breathless, and hopelessly in love.

She wriggles in her sleep, and my throat constricts at the way my body moulds to hers. Never in a million years did I think I'd feel this way.

My hand slides over her stomach, pulling her in tighter, and she lets out a faint sigh.

I love her.

The other thing I love is our days together.

Ava's playing with her increasing number of toys in her room.

We've talked so much about it, but I have the paint now, and next weekend we'll start decorating her room the way she wants it. Ginny has big plans for making it a room fit for a princess.

Now she's moved in, Ginny's also started taking turns with me cooking dinner. I've even let go and am less possessive about my kitchen. Everything I have is hers.

I smile as she walks into the living room.

"I've been thinking."

She grins. "Did it hurt?"

I roll my eyes, shaking my head. "Smartarse. I'm serious."

Ginny laughs. "I'm sorry."

"Do you think we should find a bigger place? I never planned for two people to live here, let alone three."

"I think it's fine. There's room, and the yard for Ava to play in."

I nod. "I just thought we might want to expand one day. For if we ever have more people living here."

Understanding registers on her face. "Well, there's a possibility there won't be any more people living here. So, for now, I think we should stay. Ava knows this as home, and how else is she going to sneak through into the bakery to steal a cookie?"

My jaw drops. "Do I have a cookie thief in this house?"

"To be fair, I think Mel is guilty of aiding and abetting. At least the first time."

I lean forward, crooking my index finger at her. "Come here?"

She stands, walking toward me and flopping onto the couch beside me. "What's up?"

Wrapping my arms around her, I nuzzle her cheek. "I know there's a chance we might never have a child of our own. But one day, maybe we'll try, and if it doesn't happen, it doesn't happen. If that's okay with you."

Ginny turns her head and presses a kiss to my cheek. "It's very okay with me. Once we're more settled."

"I wasn't thinking of starting tomorrow, and I don't want to put pressure on you. I know it could be a big thing to deal with."

She sighs. "I know. But I don't think I've ever had anyone in my life I'd rather try with. One day."

Ava appears in the doorway, and I raise my eyebrows at her.

"A little birdie tells me you've become a cookie thief."

"Daddy." Ava laughs, and the word hits me square in the chest.

"Is that what you're calling me now? What happened to Owen?"

Her face falls.

"It's okay. You can call me that."

She lights up. "I have two daddies."

I nod. "Yeah, you do, sweetheart."

"One makes yummy gingerbread men."

I lean back on the couch, my hand over my heart as if I've been stabbed. "You only love me for my gingerbread men."

She giggles, launching herself onto the couch and into my arms. "Silly Daddy."

I hug her tight, catching Ginny's gaze. Love's written all over her face, and my heart's more settled than ever being with my two girls.

"That's right. Silly Daddy."

I wouldn't have it any other way.

Stand alones

For the Love of Chloe

Coming 2022 Lost and Found

The Friends Duet

Loving Rowan

Three Days

The Forever Series

Something Real

The Right One

Unexpected

Chances Series

Another Chance

Taking Chances

Lifetime Series

In a Lifetime

In an Instant

In a Heartbeat

In the End

At the Start

ABOUT THE AUTHOR

Wendy Smith published as Ariadne Wayne for three years before deciding she didn't want to be someone else all the time. She's an Apple Books and Nook bestselling author, whose book In the End, written as Ariadne Wayne, was named one of Apple's best books of 2017. All her stories come with a quirky sense of humour , and she cries over everything.

Find me online
www.wendysmith.co.nz
wendy@wendysmith.co.nz